SWEET SPIRITS
OF THREE

A SWEET COVE MYSTERY

J. A. WHITING

To hear about new books and book sales, please sign up for my mailing list at:

www.jawhitingbooks.com

✺ Created with Vellum

For my family with love

1

H oliday music played in the kitchen of the Victorian while Courtney and Mr. Finch prepared some chocolate fudge.

Standing at the stove, Courtney held a wooden spoon and stirred chocolate, marshmallows, and condensed milk in a sauce pan. "I'm ready for the nuts and cherries."

"All set." Finch, an older man who had been "adopted" into the Roseland family of four sisters, limped over to the stove balancing the chopping board in his hands. He used a spatula to gently push the chopped nuts and dried cherries into the mixture.

Euclid, the huge orange Maine Coon cat, and Circe, the black feline with a white spot on her chest, perched on top of the refrigerator watching the activity.

Ellie stood at the kitchen counter using a cookie cutter to shape stars out of the buttery dough while Jenna sat at the table with a pen and a piece of paper making a list of gifts to buy for her sisters, Mr. Finch, and her new husband, Tom.

"I'm not sure what to get Tom." Jenna tapped her chin with her index finger.

"Does he need any new tools?" Ellie asked as she placed a few stars on the cookie sheet. Tom had his own house construction and renovation company.

"Maybe." Jenna fiddled with the pen. "Should the gift be something practical or something fun and unexpected?"

"I guess I'd vote for fun," Courtney said. "Tom can always buy what he needs for his business so getting him something he wouldn't get for himself would be a great gift."

"I just don't know what that could be," Jenna said. "I'll have to give it more thought."

Twenty-eight-year-old Angie Roseland, the oldest sister, entered the kitchen through the back door carrying three gift bags. Setting them down, she gave a shudder and dusted some snowflakes from the shoulders of her coat. "It's freezing outside and it's flurrying again."

Ellie shook her head. "We already have a couple of inches of snow on the ground and it is only December the first. Is this a sign of a long, snowy winter ahead?"

Jenna pushed her long, brown hair back from her face and eyed the bags. "Have you been holiday shopping already?"

"I thought I'd get a jump on it." Angie hung her coat in the back closet and went to pour herself a cup of tea. "I waited until the last minute last year and I stressed myself out. I vowed to shop early this year."

"I'm already done with my Christmas shopping," Courtney announced.

"You are?" Sitting down at the table next to Mr. Finch, Angie looked at her youngest sister with an expression of disbelief. "And here I thought I was getting my shopping done early."

"Let's put the trees up tomorrow," Courtney suggested. "I'm in the holiday spirit."

Angie glanced over to see what Mr. Finch was doing. The older man had recently rekindled an old hobby ... he'd started drawing and painting again and he was working on a charcoal picture of the

Victorian mansion decked out for Christmas on a page of his sketchpad.

"It looks great, Mr. Finch." Angie praised the man's artistry.

"I didn't realize how much I missed drawing." The man carefully made an adjustment to the roof of the house.

"What made you take it up again?" Ellie asked, slipping the cookie sheet into the oven.

Finch raised his head from his sketchbook and looked across the room, thinking. "I used to paint and draw all the time when I was a young man. The joy went out of it after my brother, Thaddeus, tried to ... well, you know what he did."

Thaddeus Finch had been a mean, nasty, greedy man who, decades ago, attempted to kill the good Mr. Finch by pushing him down a steep flight of stairs.

"About a week ago, I found myself doodling on an order form at the candy store and decided to buy a pad and some pencils and charcoal. I worked on a few sketches that night and became so immersed in the art that the hours flew by." A wide smile spread over the man's face. "It made me happy again."

"Maybe you can make each of us a drawing and give them to us as Christmas presents." Courtney used a metal spatula to evenly spread the fudge in the pan.

"I had that very idea," Finch said with a wink. "I've also purchased an easel and some oil paints and I've been working on a painting when I get home from the candy store."

"What's the subject of the painting?" Jenna asked.

Finch made eye contact with the young woman. "It's a secret."

Letting out a chuckle, Jenna joked, "Maybe we'll need to sneak over to your house some evening and peek in the windows to see this mysterious artwork."

Angie's face took on a serious look. "That reminds me. I stopped by Francine's stained glass shop earlier today. She's been working really hard trying to get all of her orders out in time. She told me she was working late the other night in the store's back room, it was almost midnight. There was a noise outside one of the windows ... she said that something about the sound made her freeze in place."

Everyone turned to Angie.

"Why did it make her freeze?" Ellie asked.

"Was she afraid someone was about to break in?" Courtney took a seat at the table next to Jenna.

"That crossed her mind," Angie told them. "Francine had the feeling someone was staring at her through the window. It was only a feeling, but she told me the sensation was strong. She was afraid to turn around and look."

"What did she do? What happened?" Jenna asked.

Angie said, "Francine stood there for a few minutes listening for any more sounds and then she got angry that someone might be looking for trouble. She stormed to the side table to grab her phone, picked up a sharp tool, and flicked the lights off in the room so whoever might be outside the window wouldn't be able to see her."

Courtney leaned forward. "Did she hear anything else? Did she see anyone?"

"She thought she saw someone at the window. When she turned off the lights in the work room, Francine thought she saw a dark figure dash away ... for a second, he was caught in the glow of the security lights at the side of the building."

"So, it was a man?" Finch asked.

"She thinks so, yes."

"Did she call the police?" Jenna questioned.

"Not right away. She forced herself to finish the piece she was working on and then packed up to go home. Before locking the door and going out to her car, she worried the man might be waiting for her outside so she called the police and asked for an escort to her car."

"That was a good idea." Ellie nodded. "Did an officer come to walk her to the car?"

"Yes, and when Francine reported what had happened, the officer told her that there have been other incidents in town of someone lurking outside windows at night staring in."

"Oh, for Pete's sake." Courtney hit the table with the palm of her hand. "What's this about? Some nut is going around town peeking in people's windows? Who would do that?"

"Someone who wants to frighten people," Jenna said with disgust.

"Hopefully," Finch said, "frightening people is this person's only goal."

"You mean it might escalate from just watching people to something more sinister?" Angie asked.

"Sometimes, the watching is only the beginning," Finch said. "At least the police are aware of what's going on. They'll keep an eye out for this person."

"I hope they catch him and lock him up." Courtney folded her arms on the table. "How many incidents of being watched have been reported?"

Angie gave a shrug. "Francine didn't know."

Ellie stood and went to remove a batch of cookies from the oven and when they had cooled, she brought a plate of them to the table. "Let's talk about something else and enjoy our evening together. I'm going to make some hot chocolate, then let's take our drinks and the cookies to the family room and relax for a while."

Jenna had been quiet for the last part of the conversation ... things felt off to her, like trouble was coming, and it left her so uneasy and anxious that she wanted to get up and head home, go to bed, and wake up to discover this nonsense about a Peeping Tom was only a bad dream.

"Can you show me some of your sketches?" Angie asked Mr. Finch in order to change the subject to something more pleasant.

"I'd be happy to, Miss Angie." Finch flipped the pages back to the start of the sketchbook and turned it so Angie could see better.

"Oh, look," Angie smiled. "It's Euclid and Circe."

Courtney swung her chair to the other side of the table. "Wow, it's a perfect likeness. I'm impressed."

"Here's one I did of Main Street." Finch turned to the next page.

"It's terrific, Mr. Finch," Angie said. "You have an amazing talent."

"I did some quick sketches of all of you." Finch showed the first one he'd done of Ellie. It was a drawing of the tall blonde standing on the front porch in profile.

Angie and Courtney praised Finch's work.

"Come see, Jenna," Courtney said to her sister.

She didn't know why, but Jenna did not want to look at the drawings. Unable to rationalize her feelings of wariness, she reluctantly got up and went to the other side of the table to stand behind Angie to look at the sketches. The one of Ellie was beautiful. Mr. Finch had done a masterful job of capturing the young woman.

"This one is of Angie." Finch flipped to the next page to show Angie in her bake shop, wearing a blue apron, piping frosting over the top of a cupcake.

While her sisters oohed over the picture, Jenna's vision began to swim and the room started to spin. The blood seemed to be draining out of her head. After closing her eyes for a moment, when she opened them again, a shot of adrenaline raced through her body. Jenna trained her gaze on the drawing, and with her heart racing, she rubbed at her eyes and blinked.

The picture of her fraternal twin sister in the sketchbook no longer depicted Angie in the bake shop.

Now a circle of bright, red light sparkled in the center of the page, and in the middle of the ring of light was a drawing ... a drawing of Angie ... in a coffin.

2

When Jenna gasped, her sisters and Finch swung around to see what had caused her alarm.

Courtney stared at her sister's pale face. "What's wrong with you?"

Sinking onto the chair, Jenna shook her head and placed a hand on the back of her neck. "I don't know. Nothing, I guess. Well, something was on the page." She gestured at Finch's sketchbook.

"Like what?" Angie watched Jenna's face and then took another glance at the drawing. "It's just a drawing of me in the bake shop."

"I...." Jenna made eye contact with her twin sister.

"Do you feel okay?" Angie asked with concern in her voice.

Finch looked from young woman to young woman trying to understand what had upset Jenna.

Ellie sat down across from Jenna and used a calm tone when she asked softly, "Did you see a ghost?" Like the other Roseland sisters and Mr. Finch, Jenna had unique paranormal powers ... she could sense and sometimes, see ghosts.

"No." Jenna didn't know how to describe what she'd seen.

"Miss Jenna," Finch said. "Is there something upsetting about my drawing?"

The brunette took a peek at the picture and saw that now, it was only a picture of Angie in her bake shop. "The first time I looked at it...." Jenna hesitated. "I saw Angie, but she wasn't in the bake shop."

Anxiety flitted over Angie's skin and her blue eyes searched her sister's face.

Courtney's eyebrow raised as she asked cautiously, "Where was she?"

With a trembling chin, Jenna whispered, "She was in a coffin."

It was like the young woman's words had struck the others across their faces ... Finch's mouth dropped open and Courtney and Ellie pressed against their seat backs with looks of horror over their faces.

Euclid stood up and let out a wild hiss.

A shot of panic raced through Angie's body, but she forced her expression to remain neutral and kept her eyes on Jenna. "What does the picture look like now?"

"It looks like what Mr. Finch intended to draw ... you baking."

"And what did you see when you looked at it initially?" Angie asked bracing for the answer.

Jenna's voice was barely audible. "It was a coffin, with you in it."

"Was there anything else in the picture?" Angie asked.

"No." Jenna shook her head.

"Was I ... dead?" Angie couldn't keep her voice from trembling.

Jenna's throat tightened. "I think so."

"Was I old?"

"No." Tears welled in Jenna's eyes.

"Was I ... the age I am now?" Angie asked.

Jenna gave a little nod.

Angie swallowed hard and turned to Mr. Finch. "What could it mean?"

Finch pushed his glasses up his nose. "I don't know what it might mean. Maybe it doesn't mean anything at all or perhaps, it was an odd synapse in

Miss Jenna's brain creating a vision much like that of an image in a strange dream."

"Why would that happen?" Courtney asked. "It's never happened before, has it?"

"Not to me." Jenna rubbed the back of her neck and tried to dismiss what she'd seen. "It was nothing. I shouldn't have said anything about it. It was a stupid thing that jumped into my brain."

Angie touched her sister's arm. "Was it really nothing?"

Jenna's stomach clenched and her eyes were heavy with sadness. "It had to be."

UNABLE TO STOP FRETTING over Jenna's upsetting vision, and feeling antsy and uneasy, Angie decided to change into running clothes and go for a jog through town. She hoped what her sister saw was what Mr. Finch had described ... a stray brain flash of some kind that caused Jenna to see an image similar to what someone sees in a dream sequence – nothing real, only something from the imagination.

But why would that image flash before Jenna's eyes? What if it *was* a picture of the future? Angie tried to banish the terrible possibility from her mind.

The streetlamps flickered on and glowed with golden light as Angie ran along the road close to the sidewalk passing the tourists and residents carrying shopping bags from their visits to the Main Street shops.

Green wreaths with red ribbons hung on doors, strings of little white lights twinkled over entrances and around window displays, and evergreens, white birch branches, and red berries stood in pots by doors or decorated the window boxes. A dusting of snow showed on the roofs of buildings.

Through restaurant windows, Angie could see people sitting at tables enjoying drinks and dinner and the company of their friends or family members. She wished she could sit happily with her loved ones unburdened by this new worry and fear of the future.

Angie jogged away from the center of town towards the neighborhoods surrounding the main street. Some snow covered front lawns and warm light glimmered inside the neat, pretty homes that lined the quiet roads away from the bustle of town.

The rhythmic movement and the exertion of

running in the cold air began to banish the nervous energy from Angie's body and her mind relaxed. Jenna's vision couldn't be a prediction of doom for the young baker, it was only an inexplicable picture that popped into her sister's brain.

A woman's scream, loud and sharp, pierced the cold air.

Angie stopped dead. Where did the sound come from?

A frightened shout came from behind the ranch-style house on the right side of the lane and Angie ran into the side yard.

"Are you okay?" she shouted facing the backyard.

"I need help." A woman in her early forties appeared at the rear corner of the house wearing jeans and a long-sleeve shirt, her brown hair pulled back from her face in a loose bun. As she punched at the phone in her hands, it fell to the ground.

Angie bent to pick it up.

"Did you see anyone around my house?" the woman demanded. "A man running away? I need to call the police." She took the phone from Angie and with shaking fingers placed the emergency call. "A man was looking in our windows again." After giving her address to the dispatcher, she disconnected the call. "I can't take this anymore. This is the third time this week."

"Someone was in the yard looking into your windows?" Angie glanced around the back of the property.

The woman pushed her hand over the top of her hair. "He was looking in at my daughter. Rachel was changing and she saw his face at the window. When she screamed, I ran out the back door to try to see him. He was gone before I stepped out." Shaking her head, she looked at Angie. "I'm Sara. Thanks for coming to help when you heard me scream."

"Someone has been looking in your windows for a week?"

Sara blew out a breath and wrapped her arms around herself to ward off the cold. "It started last Saturday." She led Angie to the back of the house. "He's been here three times. Twice early in the morning when my daughter was getting ready for school. The first time his face was at her bedroom window and the next time she saw him at the bathroom window. Now again. He was looking in the bathroom window. We hadn't pulled the shade down in there yet. We thought it was just an early morning thing, but now, I guess not," she said with disgust.

"Are there footprints under the window?" Angie asked.

"I didn't think of that. It hadn't snowed yet the first two times he was here." Sara headed to the window to inspect for footprints.

"Maybe stay here until the police arrive," Angie said. "You don't want to step where the man was standing. The officer can check for evidence, look for footprints."

Sara stopped. "Oh, right. Good idea."

"Did you or your daughter ever get a look at the man?" Angie questioned.

"I haven't seen him. Rachel is the only one he's been spying on."

"Mom?" A teenager with long, brown hair and big brown eyes opened the back door and stepped out onto the deck.

"I'm here, hon."

"Are you okay?" Rachel came down the steps. "Is he gone? Did you get a look at him?"

Sara went to hug her daughter. "He got away before I could see him. I called the police."

Rachel began to shiver from the cold. "Come back inside and get a jacket," she told her mother as she gave Angie a glance.

Sara explained who Angie was and Rachel thanked her for coming to her mother's aid.

"I screamed as I came out the door trying to scare him," Sara said. "I should have sneaked out quietly instead of giving him a warning that I was coming. Next time, I'll be more careful."

"He better not come back again." Rachel's eyes flashed with fear and anger.

"Did you get a look at him?" Angie asked the teen.

Rachel said, "I know it's a man, but I can't give much of a description. His face is up against the glass and it scares me so bad that I look away and scream. Tonight it was dark out so it made it harder to see him."

"Could you tell if he was older or a younger man?"

"I'd say a younger guy. Twenties? But I can't be sure. It always happens so fast."

"Hair color?"

"Dark?" Rachel said, unsure of her answer.

"Can you recall anything about his face?" Angie was careful not to suggest anything like a hat or a beard or glasses so as not to influence the young woman's memory.

Rachel narrowed her eyes and let out an exasperated sigh. "I don't know."

"She's sixteen years old," Sara said. "What kind of a freak would get his kicks from watching a kid through a window?" The woman gave the snow a kick with the toe of her slipper.

"Is there anyone else in the house?" Angie turned her head to look at the back of the house to see which windows were illuminated.

"It's just Rachel and me," Sara said. "My husband died about five years ago." Her shoulders sagged. "Do you think that's why this man is targeting us? Because it's only two women who are living here?"

"I don't know. That might not matter to him." From where they were standing, Angie looked over at the ground under the windows. The snow was disturbed under one of them, probably the bathroom, and a track seemed to move across the snow from that window to the woods at the back of the property.

The three women heard the doorbell ring from the front of the house.

"The police are here, Mom," Rachel said.

Angie looked from mother to daughter. "Be sure and keep the shades drawn, shut the drapes or the curtains, if you have them on the windows. Get some pepper spray ... and keep your phones close at hand." She said goodbye as Sara and Rachel went inside to open the front door for the police.

Turning to go back around the house to the street, Angie paused and took a long look at the backyard of the ranch home.

She stared at the footsteps in the snow ... and the sight of them filled her heart with dread.

3

Angie sat in a wooden chair in Police Chief Martin's cramped office in the Sweet Cove Police station reporting the incident from the previous evening while out for her jog. "When the officer rang at the front door, I headed home. I didn't see the person who was looking in the window. I only stopped because I heard the mother ... Sara ... scream."

Chief Phillip Martin, sitting opposite Angie on the other side of his old, beat-up desk with a serious expression on his face, nodded at the young woman. "This isn't the first happening. There have been multiple reports over the past two weeks of a man looking in people's windows."

"When you say *people*, do you mean only women's windows?"

"Yes."

"The other day, Francine from the stained glass shop told me she caught a man looking in the window of her backroom. She was working late at night and felt like someone was watching her. When she turned, she saw a face in the window."

"Francine called here to report the incident," the chief said.

"Is this observer targeting one particular neighborhood in town?" Angie asked.

"Unfortunately, no. Which makes it much more difficult to nab the person. He could turn up anywhere, any time." The chief picked up a pen from the top of his desk and fiddled with it. "We've never had such a thing happen in town."

"Is there anyone in town with a record of such activity? Like someone on the sex offender registry?"

"We've checked and nothing new comes up. Of course, there are tourists and visitors to town all the time. We can't know about these people unless one of them gets into trouble." The chief gave Angie a discouraged look. "We don't do background checks on every person who registers at an inn or a hotel. And some people just come for the day."

"It might not help to do that anyway," Angie said.

"The window-looker might be from another town and comes to Sweet Cove to do his...." The young woman searched her brain for the right word to use and when she thought of something, she made a disgusted face. "Observations."

"Exactly. It's not necessarily a town resident which adds another layer of difficulty to trying to find this person."

"Have there been any reports of break-ins related to this window-looker?"

"No." Worry pulled at the chief's face. "But...."

"I know what you're going to say," Angie told the chief. "There's a good chance this weirdo will graduate from just peeking in windows to something more sinister."

"That's right." The chief gave a nod. "It often doesn't stop there."

"How many reports have you had of someone looking in windows over the past two weeks?"

The chief tapped at his laptop for a few seconds. "Over the past fifteen days, there have been twenty-five occurrences."

"Twenty-five?" Angie sat straight, her voice tinged with alarm.

The chief waved her over to look at his laptop

screen. "See, the red dots on the map indicate a report of someone looking in."

Angie bent close and looked at the map of town showing on the screen. "He's all over town. There's no pattern, is there?"

"None we've been able to determine," the chief said. "He appears in the morning, late afternoon, evenings, late at night."

"What about Silver Cove and the other nearby towns?" Angie's eyes were glued to the screen. "Are they reporting something similar? Is someone peering in windows in other towns?"

The chief's shoulders sagged. "We seem to have won this person's undivided attention. Lucky us."

"Why wouldn't the window-looker spread out? Wouldn't it make it harder for him to be caught if he was making appearances over a wider area?" Angie went back to her seat.

"There could be a number of reasons why the person is only targeting Sweet Cove," the chief said. "Transportation might be an issue. The person might be traveling on foot or by bicycle. Maybe he doesn't own a car or maybe he doesn't want to use a car. If he parks near the house he's pinpointing, he is aware someone might spot his vehicle. It's much easier to arrive on foot or on a bike that he could stash in the trees or brush. No engine noise. It would be a quiet and stealthy way to arrive and depart."

"That makes sense." Angie ran her hand over her forehead. "Are there other possible reasons to target one town?"

The chief let out a sigh. "The person might have a vendetta against the town for some reason."

"Like what kind of vendetta?"

"From a perceived or actual slight of some kind," the chief said. "A fight or an argument with someone from town. The person may have been fired from a job and has turned his anger towards Sweet Cove in general. The person may have been dating a woman from town, she could have broken off with him, and now he is angry at every woman in town. There are a variety of profiles in cases like this."

"There are too many possibilities. None of the profiles are probably helpful in *catching* a Peeping Tom."

"It isn't an easy task," Chief Martin said. "Information is going out to the inns and hotels in town as well as to businesses and residential homes alerting people to this problem and offering some safety tips to keep in mind."

"What are the tips?"

"Common sense things, really. Keep your doors locked, pull drapes or shades, call the police if anything seems amiss or you spot someone suspicious lurking around."

Angie nodded. "It's important to let people know what's going on."

"If you're willing, I'd like you and your sisters and Mr. Finch to help us out."

A shiver ran down Angie's back. "How can we help?"

"I'd like you to come with me and talk to some of the residents who have reported incidents. See if we can come up with some ideas. Maybe you and your sisters might sense something at the homes and businesses where this "Observer" has been."

Angie said, "We can do that." The Roselands and Mr. Finch had some interesting paranormal powers that they used to help the police with difficult cases. "I'll talk to them about it."

"Was everyone busy today?" the chief asked. "Is that why you came to talk to me alone?"

Angie's eyes clouded. "I didn't ask the others to come."

The chief gave Angie a long look. "Why not?"

Angie hesitated, but then said, "I have something

to talk to you about. It's something unusual. It's probably nothing. I don't even know why I wanted to bring it up. It's silly."

"What is it?" the chief asked gently. "It isn't silly, if it's something that's bothering you."

Angie moved her hand in the air dismissively and was about to stand up. "I don't want to take up your time with foolishness."

"Angie." The chief's voice was firm. "I've asked you for help so many times I can't count them. If you're worried over something, then tell me about it. We help each other, even if it only means listening to a concern."

Slumping back in her seat, Angie's eyes watered. She took a deep breath and told Chief Martin about the vision Jenna had when looking at Mr. Finch's drawing. "Then Jenna saw me … dead, in a coffin. I wasn't old. She said I looked like I do now."

The chief's face paled as his eyes widened. "Did Mr. Finch see this image?"

"No." Angie shook her head. "Only Jenna."

"Has anything like this ever happened before?"

"No, this is the first time."

"Were there any clues as to what had happened to you?" The chief leaned forward.

"No clues," Angie said. "Jenna saw me in the

coffin, that was all. Nothing else, no one else was in the image." She explained how Finch had tried to brush the worry away by saying it might have been something like a dream. Mr. Finch thinks Jenna had some strange brain flash that caused her to see me ... dead. We don't really seem to have control over our dreams, they just pop into our heads. Mr. Finch thinks this was something like an awake dream."

"That sounds plausible."

"What if that *isn't* what it is?" Angie wrung her hands together in her lap. "What if Jenna is seeing something about the future, the not so distant future?"

"Has it happened only the once?" the chief asked. "Has Jenna only had the vision one time?"

"Yes." Angie held the man's eyes. "So far."

"Well, then, since it only happened once, I might agree with Mr. Finch that it was some unusual neuron flaring up, whatever that means. But it makes sense."

"Does it?" Angie asked. "I'd really like to dismiss the vision as some dream-like image, but...."

"But it worries you," the chief finished the young woman's sentence.

"Yes." The word came out of Angie's throat like the squeak of a mouse.

"It's understandable." Chief Martin scratched his head. "Is there someone, ah, more experienced in these kinds of things who you could talk to about it? Orla? What about Gloria from the hair salon?"

Both Orla and Gloria had some "skills" in the area of paranormal activity, but the chief didn't know what that constituted. In fact, Angie didn't know either.

"I could bring it up with Orla, I guess."

"She might have some ideas." The chief nodded. "Until this gets figured out, put my phone number on speed dial, the police emergency number, too. You call me, anytime, day or night. You understand? You need me, I'm there."

Angie gave a little nod.

The chief went on. "Don't go jogging in the dark or in quiet places. Stay on Main Street. Take someone with you. Stay around people. Keep your phone handy. Carry pepper spray."

"I will." Angie couldn't help a few tears of worry from forming and she brushed at them with her fingers.

The chief stared at the young woman sitting across from him. He cleared his throat. "We won't let anything happen to you, Angie. The only way someone will hurt you is over my dead body ... and

I'm telling you right now, neither one of us is leaving this earth anytime soon."

Angie wished it could all be so simple.

4

As Jenna carried a box of gemstones to her work table, she glanced up at the ceiling with a sigh wishing the noise from the third floor renovation would stop. Jenna's husband, Tom, owned a renovation company and had started the work months ago, but due to some problems with two other projects, the third floor plans to create two apartments out of the space had to be put on hold.

One of the apartments would be used by Angie and her fiancé, Josh, once they were married. The wedding date still hadn't been set. The couple was in no hurry and didn't mind that the renovation had been delayed. Work had recently started up again and even though it took place on the third floor, the noise and vibration seemed to be concentrated right over Jenna's jewelry store and workshop.

Sitting in her comfortable chair, Jenna spread the stones over a felt mat and took a look at the design she'd sketched for the necklace. She lifted a gemstone and ran her finger over the smooth finish, her mind turning away from the work in front of her and instead, thinking about what she had seen in Mr. Finch's drawing.

The image had chilled her and filled her with horror and the vision had been consuming her thoughts. Her twin sister dead? What did it mean? Was it a warning of a possibility or was it a picture of a certain future event?

A headache began to pulse in Jenna's temples as sadness and anger and misery pounded through her body. Feeling helpless and ill, the gemstone fell from her fingers and hit the mat. She looked up at the ceiling again and cursed the workers and their infuriating noise.

What can I do to protect Angie? What can we do to keep her safe? What danger is coming for her?

With tears burning against her eyelids, Jenna folded her arms on the table and rested her forehead against them.

A buzzing sound near the big window next to

her desk caused her to lift her head from her arms and she swiveled in her chair to look.

Jenna kept a large glass vase filled with sea glass on the windowsill. Over the years, she and her nana had gathered the tiny pieces of green, blue, red, brown, and white glass from the beach near the ocean river. The December sun came in through the window making the pieces of glass shimmer and gleam inside the vase.

Narrowing her eyes, Jenna held her breath as she watched the colors from the sea glass start to swirl and sparkle and turn into rays of light that lifted out of the vase and rose straight up into the air, the colored rays twirling around each other so brightly that she had to close her eyes for a few seconds.

When she lifted her eyelids, the rays of light pinged off the walls and collected in the middle of the room forming into a dancing little cyclone. Jenna raised her hand to shield her eyes from the glare.

Suddenly, the colored rays shot to the ceiling and then plunged back into the vase where they quieted … the container once again filled with the tiny pieces of sea glass.

With her heart pounding, Jenna blinked and sprang to her feet.

Where the lights had swirled in the middle of the room, there now stood a person.

"Nana," Jenna whispered as a cool breeze enveloped her.

The Roseland sisters' grandmother, petite and slender, with short silver hair and piercing blue eyes, smiled back at Jenna.

With happy tears tumbling down her cheeks, Jenna wanted to run to her grandmother and wrap her in a hug, but her feet wouldn't move no matter how hard she tried to force them forward. She reached out her arms.

Nana made eye contact with her brunette granddaughter and Jenna's body flooded with warmth and love, but in a matter of seconds, the smile dropped from Nana's lips and she lifted her hand and gestured around the room.

Silently and at the same time, the shades dropped on all eight of the huge windows in the room.

Nana took a step towards Jenna and held the young woman's eyes seemingly trying to tell her something.

The older woman's form slowly began to fade away.

"No, don't go," Jenna whispered.

Nana's body sparked and flashed ... and then she was gone.

"Come back." Jenna's voice was so soft. "Don't leave us."

Angie walked into the room with the two cats following behind her. "Why is it so dark in here? Why do you have all the shades drawn?" When she saw her sister's face, Angie rushed to her. "What's wrong? What's going on?"

Jenna took Angie hands. "Nana. She was here. I saw her."

Angie's vision began to dim and she slipped down to the floor onto her butt.

JENNA HELPED her sister to the sofa and Euclid and Circe jumped up and sniffed Angie's face.

"Nana? You saw her spirit?" Angie asked shakily.

"The sea glass started to swirl and the colors turned into rays of light and moved around the room just like when I saw her a year ago. When the rays went back into the vase, Nana was standing in the room."

"Did she ... did she speak to you?"

Jenna shook her head. "She just looked at me."

"Did she seem worried or afraid?"

"She smiled at me, then her face turned serious, and then all the shades came down."

Angie glanced around the room. "Nana caused the shades to lower?"

"Yes. I don't know how, but I know she did it. They all came down at the same time."

A cold shiver ran down Angie's back. "She didn't say anything?"

"No. I wish she did."

"I saw Chief Martin today." Angie summarized what they'd talked about.

"Why didn't you tell me you were meeting with him? I would have gone along," Jenna said.

"I needed to talk to him about my worries." Angie gave a shrug. "I needed to talk to him about what you saw in Mr. Finch's drawing. I thought he should know that I might be in danger."

Jenna reached out and pulled her sister into her arms. "No one's going to hurt you. I won't let anything happen to you. You aren't leaving me."

Euclid and Circe trilled and rubbed their faces against Angie.

Angie gave a slight nod, took in a deep breath, and swallowed to clear the tightness from her throat. "The chief asked if some of us could meet with the women who have had the man looking in on them, see if we can pick up on anything. He's going to speak with one of them tomorrow."

"Of course, we'll help. I'll go along with you," Jenna said.

"Chief Martin told me the police department was sending messages around town for people to watch for that Peeping Tom and about how to keep safe. One of the things he said to do was to keep all window shades drawn." Angie tugged at the sleeve of her sweater. "It's a coincidence, isn't it?"

"What is?"

"When Nana was here with you, she did something to lower the shades in this room." Angie looked pointedly at her sister.

Jenna's eyes widened. "She's telling us to keep safe, to draw the shades, to keep that freak from peering in our windows."

Angie's shoulders slumped and even though she didn't want to talk about it, she asked, "Could this Peeping Tom have something to do with your vision?"

Jenna stared at her sister, her lower lip trembling, but she didn't say anything.

"Am I in danger from this man?" Angie asked.

"No one's been looking in our windows," Jenna managed weakly.

"Yet." Angie looked around the room at the shades covering the windows. "Have you had any other visions?"

Jenna looked down. "I haven't looked at any more of Mr. Finch's drawings."

"I think you should. Even though it's hard and upsetting."

"Mr. Finch was so upset I think he's stopped drawing," Jenna said.

Angie pushed her shoulders back and sat up straighter. "We can't put our heads in the sand. Honestly? I'm terrified, but we need to have as much information as possible, if ... if I'm going to keep your vision from becoming a reality. I refuse to believe the future is set in stone. What you saw *might* happen. I'm going to fight like heck to make sure it doesn't happen."

Jenna lifted her eyes to her sister. "Well, I'll be standing right beside you in this, and so will the others. That's how we're going to face this ... together ... and that's how we're going to win."

The corners of Angie's mouth turned up. "We'll meet with the people who have been victimized by this Peeping Tom and we'll gather as much information as possible. And we need Mr. Finch to draw again so that you can look at the pictures and try to find clues."

Euclid squished onto the sofa in between the two sisters and Circe settled on Angie's lap and gave the young woman's hand a lick.

"The cats will help, too." Jenna smiled. "Let's call Mr. Finch and tell him we need him to start drawing again."

Courtney and Ellie came into Jenna's studio.

"Here you are," Ellie said. "We were looking for you."

"We were wondering where you two were hiding out." Courtney plopped into an easy chair. "What's cookin'?"

"Plenty," Jenna said with a smile.

"Jenna had a visitor a few minutes ago," Angie told them.

Ellie's face paled. "The Peeping Tom? He looked in the window?"

"No," Jenna said. "Quite the opposite. It was someone we all know, and love with all our hearts."

Courtney's eyes went wide and she swung her

legs off the arm of the chair. She stared at Jenna. "Nana?" she whispered.

When Jenna gave a nod, the youngest Roseland sister jumped to her feet and let out a happy whoop of joy.

5

A ngie had closed the bake shop for the day, showered and changed, and now stood in the foyer of the Victorian waiting for Jenna. The December sun was already low in the sky and in two hours, it would be dark. Although she loved the holiday season, Angie missed the long, warm days of summer, her favorite time of year.

Angie's heart skipped a beat. Would she still be here in the summer?

"Hello." A man's voice spoke and Angie turned to see a medium-height, medium build man in his fifties descending the elaborately carved wooden staircase. "Are you a guest here? I'm Marvin Oates." He extended his hand to shake.

"I'm Angie Roseland. I live here. Actually, I'm

living in the carriage house out back while renovations are being done on the third floor."

"You're Ellie's sister, then?"

Angie nodded.

"Your sister warned me about the renovation work being done in case I wanted to change my reservation, but it hasn't bothered me at all. And your sister was kind enough to lower the daily room rate in the event the noise was a problem. It hasn't been a concern at all. You have a beautiful home. I love this town."

Angie asked where the man was from.

"I'm from Washington, D.C. My wife passed away last year and I'm traveling to keep busy. The seacoast area is magnificent, the history, the museums, the scenery."

A woman spoke from the dining room. "And the Peeping Tom."

"What's that?" Mr. Oates asked.

A slender woman in her fifties with dark chin-length hair dressed in a wool skirt and a cardigan stepped into the foyer carrying a cup of coffee. "There's a Peeping Tom running around town scaring people to death. Haven't you heard?"

"I haven't, no." Oates shook his head.

"Not surprised." The woman took a swallow of

her coffee. "Being a man, you wouldn't be concerned about such a thing." Turning her attention to Angie, she said, "I'm Elizabeth Winters. I'm staying here at the inn for a week, maybe more. You're Ellie's sister?"

Angie introduced herself. "Are you here on business?"

"Oh, gosh, no," Ms. Winters said. "I needed a break from business. I'm a vice president at a financial firm in Boston. At this time of year, I like to get away for a two- or three-week break. I was at an inn in Salem last week. I was feeling rundown and out of sorts so I took the time off to slow down and get in the holiday spirit."

"Is it working?" Oates asked.

"Is what working?" Ms. Winters asked.

"Getting away from it all. Are you feeling in a holiday mood now?"

"Oh, I'm starting to. I only arrived on the North Shore last week. It takes time to learn to relax and get out of that rush-rush mode." Ms. Winters looked at Angie. "The Victorian's decorations are lovely."

"We'll be putting trees up in a few days," Angie said. "And we'll be hosting drinks and appetizers out by the fire pit. Ellie will put a notice in your rooms to let you know the date and time."

"Sounds terrific," Oates said.

"I look forward to it," Ms. Winters said.

Footsteps on the staircase caused Angie to look up. The two construction workers stepped down to the foyer.

Ronald said to Angie, "All done for the day. Tom plans to give you a tour of the apartments the day after tomorrow. It's coming out great, if I do say so myself." The man was just under six feet with brown hair and brown eyes. He'd just started working for Tom's company about two months ago.

The other worker, Lance, a good-looking man, was in his late twenties, similar in height and coloring to Ronald, but with sharper facial features and a long skinny neck with a large Adam's apple. He was generally shy and quiet. Tom said he was a good worker and had quality construction and renovation skills.

"I'm looking forward to seeing the work," Angie said. "I'll be happy to move in when it's all done. My sister and I are sharing one of the carriage house apartments and we're both eager to get back into the Victorian."

Jenna hurried into the foyer from the hall. "Sorry I'm late," she told Angie.

After taking a few minutes to chat with the guests and with Ronald and Lance, Jenna and Angie left the house to meet Chief Martin and the woman who had the unfortunate experience of the man looking in her windows.

BELLA MASTERS, in her late fifties with short blond hair and an athletic build, led the chief, Jenna, and Angie into her rear yard and pointed to a window on the first floor. "That's where he was, standing right outside that window. I was in the room I use as an office working at my desk. It was about 8pm. I was engrossed in my work when something, I don't know what it was exactly, made me look to the window. There he was. I screamed. It was so unexpected and strange to see someone staring at me that the scream just came out … an instinctive reaction, I suppose."

Jenna nodded. "I must be a natural instinct to scream, maybe to try and frighten the person away."

"What happened next?" Chief Martin had spoken with Bella Masters a few days ago, but wanted her to recount the experience for Jenna and Angie.

"He made eye contact with me. Isn't that bold? It was almost like he was daring me to stop him." Bella put a hand on her hip. "The nerve of this idiot."

"Did you only see him just that once?" Jenna asked.

"Twice. He came back the next night. I'd been working in the den again, with the shade pulled down this time, I might add. I went to the kitchen to make some tea. When I turned to the fridge, there he was again, at the window at the back door." Bella's face took on a look of disgust.

"What happened?" Jenna asked. "Did he run when he saw you looking at him?"

Bella narrowed her eyes. "He sure did. When I pulled this out." The woman put her hand into the pocket of her jacket and removed a handgun.

Angie stared in surprise.

"I have a license to carry. I know how to handle a gun. I think my visitor had a little shock when I pointed this at him." A little smile lifted Bella's lips. "I don't expect him to return."

"I sure wouldn't come back if I was him." Even though it was pointed at the ground, Jenna stepped a little to her left to be certain she wasn't lined up with the muzzle of the gun.

"I'd pick someone who didn't have a weapon," Angie said.

"We've talked about the gun," the chief said. "It most likely scared off the man, but...." He hesitated.

Bella spoke up. "Chief Martin said that sometimes, in cases like this, the kook might feel threatened by my weapon, like I'm challenging him or daring him or some such thing, which makes him angry and makes him want to get back at me."

Angie and Jenna turned their attention to the chief.

"So what does that mean?" Jenna asked. "Showing the weapon to the man makes him come back?"

The chief gave a nod. "Sometimes, it pushes the perpetrator to become emboldened. It can cause an escalation in behavior."

"When did this happen?" Angie questioned. "When was the last time he was here?"

"The fool showed up here two days ago," Bella said as she slipped the gun back into her pocket.

"You said the man made eye contact with you," Angie said. "Can you describe his appearance?"

Bella sighed. "Both times, it was a quick look, even though he held my gaze, it only lasted for a half-second or so. It was dark, the face was in shadow. He had on a hat, a knitted winter type hat pulled down over his head." She lifted her hand to the top of her eyebrows. "It was pulled down to here. I couldn't see his hair."

"Could you see what he was wearing?" Jenna asked.

"A winter jacket, dark color."

"Anything about the face that stood out?"

Bella said, "He looked like any guy, a regular face, no facial hair. Remember, it happened quick. I was shocked, a rush of panic went through me. I don't think the senses register much when something like this happens. The guy has surprise on his side."

"When you think back on the night," Angie said, "Does anything seem familiar about the man? Even in the most general way?"

Bella didn't answer right away. She was thinking it over, pulling the images from her brain. "Really, nothing. I don't recall seeing the man before those two nights."

"Do you have family?" Jenna asked.

"My kids live in Boston. I have the house to myself."

"Husband or partner living with you?"

"My husband died six years ago," Bella said.

"Do you have a dog?"

"No pets. It's just me in the house." Bella frowned. "You think this guy stalked me? Cased the house to see if I lived alone?"

"I wouldn't be surprised," the chief said. "The perpetrator would expect women living by themselves, or with kids, to be an easier mark than someone living with men."

"Even a woman with a gun?" Bella cocked her head to the side in question.

"Depends on the criminal," the chief said with a serious tone in his voice. He reviewed with Bella ways to stay safe and went over what to do in the event the man returned.

On the way back to the car, Jenna said, "It wasn't all that helpful. The window-looker is an average guy with a hat yanked down over his head. It's cold and snowy and dark. Everyone is wearing heavy jackets and hats. Every man in Sweet Cove fits that description."

"I didn't sense anything about the man at the window," Angie said quietly. "I only picked up on Bella's lingering anger and residual fear."

"Same with me," Jenna said.

"Have there been any sightings since the last night the looker was at Bella's place?" Angie asked.

"Yeah," the chief opened the door to the cruiser for the young women. "Last evening. That's where we're headed now. To talk to the woman who had the *visitor* come to her house last night. Her incident was different than the other people's experiences."

"How so?" A flutter of anxiety washed down Angie's back.

"Last evening," Chief Martin told them, "the perpetrator was *inside* the house."

Jenna gasped and Angie's heart dropped into her stomach.

6

Alice Post opened the door to Angie, Jenna, and Chief Martin. She was petite and slim, slightly stooped, with white hair and watery blue eyes. The chief told the sisters that Alice was in her late eighties. A gray cat rubbed against the woman's legs.

"Come in, please." Alice led the visitors to her sitting room with modern, but comfortable furniture, the walls painted a soft cream color, and three big windows overlooking the side yard. "Have a seat."

The coffee table had a platter of cheese and crackers, cut-up veggies, and small vanilla cookies. A silver pot of tea stood next to cups and saucers. Alice poured for everyone and handed them the cups.

"I'm very glad you came to speak with me." Alice

smiled warmly at Angie and Jenna. "I'll do whatever I can to help another person avoid the scare I had last night. You might think that because I'm just a block from Main Street, I might be immune to the antics of a criminal, but that idea would be false, as I have recently learned."

"Can you tell us what happened last night?" Angie asked.

"I'd be happy to. A friend left after an afternoon visit. We had a very nice time talking with one another. Shortly after she left, I made and ate my dinner. I fed my cat, Robby." Alice's cat was curled on the woman's lap, purring. "I was feeling tired so I went to my room and got into bed with the intention of reading for a few hours. I dozed off with the lamp by my bed still on." Alice sighed and lifted her tea cup to her lips. "I woke up, but remained quiet and still. I don't know what tipped me off to an intruder, but I sensed someone in the house, so I listened and didn't move."

Jenna leaned forward. "What did you do?"

Alice folded her hands in her lap. "I keep pepper spray and a knife under my pillow. It's a crazy world and I live alone with my cat so I want to be able to defend myself." The older woman batted at the air. "Oh, I know I'm an old woman, but if someone is going to attack me, I won't make it easy for them."

Angie smiled.

"So pretending I was still asleep, I reached under the pillow and took hold of my weapons." Alice paused for a few seconds reliving the terror of the event. "My heart was pounding so fast I wouldn't have been surprised if I'd had a heart attack right there in my bed. I heard a creak from the floorboards. The man was in my room. I opened my eyes and slowly pushed myself up to face him."

"He was in your room?" Jenna asked breathlessly.

"He sure was. I stared at him. He didn't move. After a few moments, I spoke. I had to be sure my voice was steady and firm."

"What did you say?" Jenna questioned.

"I told him that this was my house and he had not been invited in. I told him I wanted him to leave. I said I didn't have any idea why he had entered my home and that the reason was immaterial to me. He needed to go." Alice patted her gray cat. "Robby, here, was on top of my dresser. He hissed at the man. I worried the man would try to hurt Robby so I got ready to spring out of bed and let him have the pepper spray right in the face."

Angie stared at the woman. "What did the man do?"

"He looked at Robby, turned back to me, and left my room. I could hear him moving down the hall to the kitchen. The back door opened and closed. He was gone."

"He just left?" Jenna was stunned. "Did he say anything?"

"Not a word. It was quite a strange encounter."

Angie glanced at the chief. "Were there footprints at the backdoor?"

"Yes," the chief said. "They are similar in size and tread to what we've found at the other homes and businesses."

"He was in your room ... the light was on. Did you get a good look at him? Can you describe the man's appearance?" Angie waited hopefully for Alice's reply.

"I'm sorry to say I have very little to contribute to a description. The man had one of those ski masks on, you know the kind, the knitted ones that pull over the face with eye holes. I can't even tell you the color of his hair." Alice shook her head. "He wore jeans and a heavy black jacket, the kind that looks like a ski jacket. I couldn't see what he had on his feet, boots, I'd guess."

"Was he tall?"

"I would say the man was of medium height and build," Alice said.

"Anything about his hands?" Angie clutched at straws.

"He kept his hands in his pockets."

"What about the way he moved? Did he seem older, young?"

"He was definitely not old," Alice said. "He moved with ease. He gave the impression of being fairly fit, in his thirties or forties? The man could have been older than that, but if that is the case, then the person is athletic and keeps himself in shape."

Angie looked to the chief again. "Is it strange that the man came into the house, didn't do anything, and left?"

Chief Martin cleared his throat. "It isn't, but I will say that reports on such behavior might indicate that this is an escalation in the man's actions. This was most likely the first time our Peeping Tom took steps to enter a home. He may do it again." The chief modified his statement. "He will probably break into a home and repeat what he did here with Alice."

"An escalation?" Angie asked. "So this man is moving from watching from outside windows to entering homes in order to surprise and frighten a victim."

"Yes," the chief said.

"And then the next step in the escalation will be attacking the homeowner?" Angie held her breath.

"Not always, but when a person moves from outside to inside, we expect his behavior will eventually advance to an attack. Most Peeping Toms remain at the first level, just watching through windows."

"So this development is very concerning," Jenna pointed out.

"It sure is," the chief said in a quiet voice.

"I don't want to say this," Angie said, "but what if the criminal returns? Is pepper spray, a knife, and a hissing cat going to dissuade him from taking the next step?" She looked over at Alice. "You're a brave woman, but you're here alone. Is there someone you can stay with for a while?"

Alice said, "I have a company coming tomorrow to install a security system. It will be connected with the police station. If the house is broken into, a message will be sent to the Sweet Cove police."

"What about tonight?" Angie asked. "Can you stay with someone until the security system is installed?"

Alice gave a nod. "I have every intention of living a very long life and I don't believe in taking chances. I have made plans to go to my friend's house. My cat and I will be staying with her this evening."

Angie breathed a sigh of relief. "I'm glad. I think that's smart."

"Would you mind if we had a look at your bedroom?" Jenna asked. "Could you show us the back door, too, and lead us down the hall the way the intruder probably came in?"

Angie's stomach clenched.

"We should look outside as well." Jenna turned to the chief. "Were footprints visible near the house? Is there evidence that the man looked through the windows before entering?"

"It appears the man went from window to window at the back of the house before getting in," Chief Martin said.

"How did he get in?" Angie questioned.

"He picked the lock," the chief said. "It was a simple keyed knob. Quite easy to pick."

"All the locks are going to be changed tomorrow as well," Alice said with a huff. "To something more complicated to pick."

Angie thought about all the locks on the doors and windows of the Victorian and made a mental note to have a locksmith come out to the house to have a look at them. She thought it might be worth having the locks upgraded.

"Come this way and I'll show you the kitchen and the back door." Alice led the way down the hall with Robby, the cat, following behind. When they entered a small, but upgraded kitchen, Alice pointed out the door where the perpetrator entered and exited. "This is the hallway to the bedroom."

The three investigators walked down the hall to the bedroom and Angie and Jenna stood at the threshold peering in.

"Those two bedroom windows face the back of the property?" Angie asked.

"That's right," Alice said.

"The man must have walked around behind the house, saw this room had a light on, and decided to enter the home and head for this room." Jenna looked to Chief Martin for confirmation.

The chief gave a nod. "Alice tells us the rest of the rooms were dark so the light on in here indicated to the man that this room was most likely occupied."

Angie and Jenna stood like soldiers, still and quiet, gazing around the bedroom space trying to pick up on anything that might have lingered on the air from the man's visit.

Angie could smell a faint scent, a man's presence, a nervousness that caused the man to sweat. The odor remained in the room, however slight.

"Was he standing here?" Jenna asked and adjusted her position to be exactly where the intruder had stood.

Alice didn't say anything, just nodded.

The chief suggested to Alice that they leave the two young women alone to look around so he and the older woman returned to the kitchen.

Jenna leaned closer to her sister and whispered. "I sense a mixture of emotions in this room. I also get the feeling the intruder has been practicing by watching through people's windows and by breaking into this house."

"What's he practicing for?" Angie asked softly, but had a sinking feeling she already knew the answer.

"He's becoming bolder." Jenna took her sister's hand and squeezed. "Is his real goal to harm someone?"

7

"I'm so happy Nana showed up the other day." Courtney and Mr. Finch were making chocolate truffles. "It's been at least a year since Jenna has seen her. I bet she showed up to warn us about the Peeping Tom."

"There have been other times of danger though," Finch said. "Why did your nana appear because of the Peeping Tom and not at other times to give you warnings?"

Ellie added cookies and slices of banana bread to the snack platter for the B and B guests. "That's a good observation, Mr. Finch. What's different this time? Why did Jenna see Nana now? Is it a coincidence Nana showed up? Maybe it has nothing to do with this criminal."

"But, the shades went down in the room when

Nana appeared, all by themselves and all at the same time," Jenna said as she added some water to the stock pot on the stove. "Nana did that, she made the shades lower. It has to be because of the Peeping Tom tormenting the town."

Holding the wooden spoon over the pot, she turned her head to the others. "Is the intruder in this case the person who is going to try and hurt Angie? Or is it someone else? I've been worrying that we're going to overlook the real menace to Angie by concentrating on the wrong person."

"Oh." Ellie's eyes widened. "We've been assuming the danger to Angie is from this Peeping Tom. He started his antics around the time Jenna saw the vision in Mr. Finch's drawing."

Angie walked into the kitchen with Euclid and Circe following behind. Ever since Jenna's vision of Angie in a coffin, the two fine felines had been keeping close to the oldest Roseland sister.

Angie said, "I'm keeping all options open. Maybe I need to be on guard against the Peeping Tom, but maybe he isn't a danger to me at all. It could be someone else I need to watch out for. At the moment, I'm not trusting anyone I don't know well."

"You're handling this very well," Ellie noted. "If I was the one in the vision, I'd be unable to leave the house ... I wouldn't be able to function. I'd be curled up in a ball in my bed."

"You wouldn't be like that." Angie smiled at her sister. "You don't like the paranormal, but when danger threatens, you are a fierce warrior. You've saved us from harm at least twice. Having you with me makes me feel safer."

Ellie blinked. "I never feel like a warrior. I mostly feel like a coward."

"Being brave isn't the absence of fear, Miss Ellie, it is doing what's necessary despite the fear," Finch told the young woman. "And you have never wavered in the face of danger when it has pinned us to the wall."

Angie's and Finch's words caused a shy smile to form over Ellie's mouth. "I guess I would just prefer that danger goes elsewhere and leaves us all alone."

Chuckles filled the air.

"I believe we would all second that sentiment, Miss Ellie," Finch said.

The aroma of simmering peanut and vegetable soup filled the air and Jenna stirred the mixture with the spoon. "I'm making soup for dinner. Maybe we can have grilled cheese and tomato sandwiches to go with it."

"Sounds great." Angie took a seat next to Finch at the kitchen island. "Have you been drawing?"

Finch paused in rolling the truffles in chocolate powder. "I have. I was reluctant initially when Miss Jenna asked me to continue, but if she sees something in the artwork that can keep you safe, then I will draw all day long if that will help us."

"Did you bring your sketchpad?" Angie couldn't help a shiver of fear from running over her skin.

"I did." Finch nodded to the kitchen table where the pad was pushed to one side.

"Jenna will look at the pictures after dinner." Angie glanced over to her twin to see Jenna's eyes heavy with worry so she changed the topic of conversation to something lighter. "Later tonight, Tom is going to give us a tour of the renovations on the two apartments upstairs. I can't wait to see how everything looks so far. Josh is coming for dinner and to see what Tom's workers have done."

Courtney formed the next batch of the chocolate mixture into truffles. "Those two guys give me the creeps."

"Tom's employees?" Jenna asked. "Why?"

"They give off some odd vibe I don't like." Courtney made a face. "I don't trust them. I wish Tom would put them on some other project and bring back the other two guys who started the renovation work."

Jenna said, "You need to tell Tom your concerns. He'll be here in an hour. Bring it up with him. He'll want to know."

"That's the problem though," Courtney said. "There isn't anything I can pinpoint, it's nothing overt. It's just something I feel when I see them."

Jenna made eye contact with the youngest sister. "Tom gets us, he understands. He knows we pick up on things that other people can't. He'll take your concerns seriously."

"Maybe," Courtney muttered. "I don't want to get anyone into trouble over my *feelings*."

"Talk to Tom anyway," Jenna said. "He'll want to know how you feel."

Angie said, "You know, when I was talking to two of the B and B guests in the foyer, the renovators came down to leave for the day. That young one, Lance, something about him made me feel uncomfortable."

Courtney perked up. "That's exactly it. It's the way he looks at you, isn't it? It's kind of creepy."

"Maybe he just doesn't have very good social skills," Ellie offered.

The discussion was tabled until Tom arrived and

Jenna encouraged Courtney and Angie to alert him to their concerns about Lance.

~

COURTNEY EXPLAINED to Tom that there wasn't anything in particular that the man did, it was subtle things that made her feel uneasy when he was around. Angie admitted to feeling the same way.

"Lance has only been in my employment for a short time, about three weeks or so," Tom said sitting at the dining room table with the family. "I don't know him well. He came with good experience and recommendations. He'd been working with a well-known renovation company up in Maine."

"Why did he leave there?" Finch asked.

"Lance told me he wanted to be back in Massachusetts. He'd grown up here. He didn't like being so far north. I hired him right away. We've got so many projects going on, I may have bit off more than we can chew. That's why the delay with the apartments here." Tom smiled. "I figured I could push out a family member's timeline easier than a client's. The family is more forgiving."

Josh said, "Angie and I don't mind at all. The

apartments don't have to be completed by a certain time. Do what you need to do for your business."

"Wait a minute," Courtney kidded. "I've been displaced from my room upstairs into the carriage house. I vote to inconvenience one of your clients so you can finish my living space in the Victorian."

Tom chuckled. "Since Josh and Angie are the ones paying for the renovations, you'll have to take up your complaint with them."

"Don't you like sharing the carriage house apartment with me?" Angie teased her sister.

"I'm fine with being your roommate, sis, but I like being here in the house where all the action is," Courtney said.

After finishing their meals of soup and sandwiches, the family cleaned up the dishes and headed up the stairs to the third floor to see the renovation work. Courtney took Mr. Finch's arm to help him navigate the staircase.

"Nothing is complete," Tom said. "It's mostly studs and open walls, but I'm hoping you can check it out and get a mental vision of what's planned. It's easier to make changes now rather than when the walls go up."

Both Jenna and Angie cringed at the word *vision*

since it reminded them of Jenna seeing the image of her twin in a coffin.

Tom led the group through the spaces explaining the details and how it would look when finished.

"It seems enormous," Courtney said with a grin. "It's great."

"The open walls give the area a really spacious feel," Tom said. "Once the walls go up, it won't give the impression of being so large."

"It's still a big apartment," Courtney said glancing at Angie and Josh. "Thanks, you two."

"Here is where the bedrooms will be," Tom gestured. "The office will be at the end of the hall." He led the group back into the living spaces. "We're standing in the living room-dining room and along that wall will be the kitchen with a large island separating the spaces."

"We love it," Angie told her brother-in-law. "We're lucky to have you in the family." Giving Tom a wink, she added, "And not just because of your construction skills."

"Why don't we head downstairs for dessert and coffee," Ellie said when the tour was over.

Everyone headed for the staircase when Euclid

let out a hiss and the family turned to see what was bothering the big orange boy.

Circe stood next to a tool box left behind by the workers. She gently moved her paws over something inside the box and lifted it out with her mouth. The small black cat padded towards Angie and when she reached the young woman's feet, the cat placed the object on the floor.

"What's this, little one?" Angie bent to see.

"At least, it's not a mouse," Ellie said with relief.

"What is it, sis?" Courtney moved closer to her sister.

"It's a newspaper clipping." Angie stared at the paper in her hand and a gasp slipped from her throat. "It's a picture of me in the bake shop when I moved the store into the Victorian."

Josh took the paper from his fiancée. "It's from the news story they did on you about helping on the case to figure out what happened to the Professor and who killed her. This clipping was in that tool-box? Why?"

"Angie," Jenna said. She stood near the toolbox leaning down to look at it. "These are Lance's tools. His name is written on the side of the box."

A cold chill ran down Angie's back.

8

Courtney was steaming. "Why would Lance have a newspaper clipping about you in his toolbox?"

"There's probably an innocent explanation." Angie sat at the kitchen island with her chin in her hand looking exhausted.

"I'll have a talk with him tomorrow." Tom's face looked tense and angry.

"I wonder if you should," Jenna said. "It might be best to put the clipping back in his toolbox and pretend we never found it. We'll all keep an eye on Lance and see if he's up to anything. Talking to him about it will make him cautious and careful. If he has something criminal in mind, let's catch him at it so he can go to jail."

Fiddling with a strand of her long blond hair,

Ellie considered Jenna's suggestion. "That might be a good idea. If we ask about the clipping, it will warn Lance we're suspicious of him. He could still plan to do something to Angie, but he'll be more secretive about it. If Tom moves Lance to a different project or fires him, then we'll lose sight of him. It might be better to keep him under our watchful eyes."

Josh put his arm around Angie's shoulders. "What do you think? What do you want to do?"

Angie's mind was a jumble of thoughts and emotions. Finally, she blew out a long breath. "Don't say anything to him. Let's watch him ... carefully ... for now. Are you okay with that, Tom?"

"Whatever keeps you safe is fine by me." Tom made eye contact with the oldest Roseland sister. "I might adjust the projects' schedules so I can work here more often. That way, I can keep my eye on Lance, maybe get an idea of what he's up to."

Angie turned her attention to Mr. Finch. "Do you think this idea is okay?"

Finch stroked his chin. "As long as you aren't alone here when Lance is in the house, then, yes, I think alerting him to our concerns might make figuring out his intentions more difficult. Keeping the young man close is in our best interests."

After more discussion and final agreement from

everyone not to alert Lance to the discovery of the news clipping, Josh left to return to the resort and Tom headed for the third floor to check the renovation work more closely.

"Have you seen Nana again?" Courtney asked Jenna.

Jenna shook her head slowly. "I wish she'd come back and give us some clues."

"I bet she will," Ellie tried to use a cheerful tone. "I bet you'll see her again soon."

The sisters and Mr. Finch were on edge because Jenna was going to look through the man's sketchbook to see if any new visions came to her.

Jenna stood. "Shall we go ahead with our plan? I've been on edge all day. Can we, please, get it over with?"

Angie hated to see her sister in distress, but there wasn't any way to avoid the task. "The family room? Would you rather the rest of us didn't come in?"

"I want you all with me." Jenna's facial expression showed a mix of worry and fear.

They moved into the family room at the back of the house with the cats accompanying them. Jenna and Mr. Finch sat on the sofa with the sketchbook in Finch's lap. Circe jumped up and snuggled next to Jenna.

Courtney took the easy chair with Euclid squeezing in beside her and Ellie and Angie sat on the opposite sofa.

Mr. Finch handed the sketchbook to the young woman. "I did quite a few drawings. I allowed my mind to wander and just took my charcoal pencil and drew as quickly as I could. I drew whatever popped into my head, sort of like a stream of consciousness."

Jenna took a deep breath and slowly turned the pages. Looking at the pictures, she began to relax as she admired Finch's artistic talent and the images he'd sketched of the town, the Victorian, the house's gardens, the cats, and the sisters. Jenna couldn't help but smile at the drawing of Circe asleep on Tom's chest while the man napped in the sunroom one afternoon.

Turning the page, Jenna's eyes widened at the picture of the Sweet Cove Fourth of July celebration. It was a scene of the food vendors and craft booths and of people walking along enjoying the sunshine and the company of friends and family as they strolled through the center of town. Flags flew, a band played on the common, children held long strings attached to balloons, dogs walked alongside their owners.

Jenna picked out Courtney and Finch selling candy at their booth and she spotted Angie near her bake shop booth handing a cupcake to a customer. The drawing brought back memories of last year's town festival and all the fun they'd had selling their wares and interacting with the townspeople and tourists.

Jenna leaned closer to see who else Mr. Finch had included in the picture. She found Chief Martin and his wife and then she spotted Tom and Josh standing on the common.

Jenna's attention was drawn back to Angie working at her bake shop booth. A flash of light seemed to burst inside her head and she closed her eyes for a second.

When she opened them, a tiny ring of fire seemed to glow from the drawing. Jenna blinked. In the center of the ring of fire, stood a little girl with honey-blond hair. She looked to be about five years old. The girl had big blue eyes and had on blue shorts and a light blue tank top. She held a chocolate cupcake in her hand and was smiling up at Angie with a wide grin.

Suddenly, the little girl turned in the drawing and looked out at Jenna. Her big eyes bore into the eyes of the young woman staring into the picture.

The little girl dropped her cupcake and held both arms out to Jenna as if asking for her help. A tear ran down her cheek, and then she was gone.

Jenna gasped and dropped the sketchbook onto her lap.

Angie jumped to her feet and hurried over to her sister.

"You saw something, Miss Jenna?" Finch asked with concern.

Jenna opened her mouth, but she only stammered and blinked and then a torrent of tears fell from her eyes.

Angie knelt in front her sister and wrapped her arms around her. "It's okay. You're here with us. It's over."

Jenna breathed deeply and patted at her cheeks, embarrassed. "I ... I'm okay." She swallowed and took long breaths in and out.

"Can you tell us what you saw?" Courtney leaned forward in her chair. Euclid stood on the arm of the chair, his eyes locked onto Jenna.

Circe nudged at Jenna's arm and the young woman pulled the cat into her lap so she could run her hand over the soft, black fur.

"You saw something?" Angie was still kneeling on the floor.

Jenna gave a nod.

"Was it the coffin again?" Angie asked in a whispered tone.

"No. It was in Mr. Finch's drawing of the Fourth of July festival." Jenna flipped to the page and showed Angie. "Here you are in your booth selling cupcakes."

Angie leaned close to see.

Jenna swallowed again and touched her finger to the picture. "It was right here. Right behind you."

"What was it?" Angie asked. "There's just grass there."

"Someone was standing in that spot right behind you." Jenna moved her shaking hand over her face.

"Someone menacing?" Ellie asked slowly.

"No." Jenna's chest rose and fell rapidly. "It...." Her thoughts were racing as she tried to make sense of what she'd seen.

Courtney left the room and returned with a glass of water. Jenna drank it down in several gulps.

"Can you tell us?" Angie asked. "Or do you want to rest a little first?"

"I'm okay." It felt like all of Jenna's energy had drained out of her body and she could barely place the glass down on the side table. After clearing her throat, she sat straight trying to collect herself.

"Right here in the drawing ... right behind Angie. There was a little girl. She was holding one of your cupcakes."

"I didn't draw a little girl," Finch clarified, "so it was a vision of her that you saw."

Jenna gave a nod. "A ring of fire encircled the little girl."

"What happened?" Courtney looked ready to jump out of her skin. "Did the little girl just stand there?"

"She looked right into my eyes." Jenna's heart raced. "She dropped her cupcake."

Angie stared, her own heart racing in anticipation.

"She started to cry."

No one said a word, they waited for Jenna to tell what she'd seen in her own time.

Rubbing her temple, Jenna continued. "The little girl reached out to me. She reached her hands out to me. She wanted my help."

"Did she speak?" Angie asked.

"No, she just reached out to me. She was happy at first, and then she started to cry."

"Did you recognize the girl?" Finch asked gently. "Do you know who she is?"

"I didn't recognize her, but I think I know who

she is," Jenna said, reaching for Angie's hands. "She had your hair color, your blue eyes, the shape of your face … and Josh's smile."

Angie's eyes grew wide.

Jenna squeezed her sister's hands. "I think she's your daughter, Angie. I think she's the daughter you'll have one day."

T he group sat in stunned silence.

"My daughter?" Angie said softly, as a powerful urge to protect the little girl surged through her.

"Why was the little girl crying?" As soon as the words left her mouth, Ellie's face changed to an expression of understanding and then to one of fear.

Angie asked, "She seemed to be asking you for help?"

Jenna nodded and ran the back of her hand over her eyes.

Angie sat down on the floor in front of her sister and crossed her legs. "Another spirit come to warn me."

"Your nana came from the past and now this little girl from the future," Mr. Finch observed.

"Do you know her name?" Angie asked.

"No," Jenna answered.

"Tell me again what she looked like," Angie requested.

Jenna gave her sister a slight smile. "She was cute. Her hair came to her chin. It was the same color as yours and Courtney's. Her eyes were blue and the shape of them looked just like yours. She smiled like Josh does, with a little dimple right here." Jenna touched her face to show where the dimple was located. "She looked athletic, and spunky."

The group chuckled while imagining the little girl that Angie would have one day.

"Can she bake?" Courtney joked.

"I'm sure she probably can," Jenna smiled. "Considering who her mother is."

The two cats trilled.

Angie's eyes grew dark. "So this child appeared to you in Mr. Finch's drawing. It's pretty clear that she came to warn me about an unknown danger. She cried and reached out to you. If something happens to me and...." Angie cleared her throat. "And I die, this little child will never be born."

Jenna bit her lower lip.

"Did she give you any indication what it is I should be afraid of?" Angie asked.

"No, I only know she wanted me to help."

Courtney stood up and began pacing around the room. "Gosh, I wish Nana would come back and talk to Jenna. I wish this little girl would tell Jenna what we need to watch for to keep Angie safe. Why are spirits so difficult?"

Ellie came over and sat next to Mr. Finch. "Have you ever daydreamed about kids?" she asked Angie. "Have you ever thought about what you would name the child if you and Josh ever had a daughter?"

Angie wrapped her arms around her legs and pulled them close to her chest. "Yeah, I have. Actually, Josh and I kidded around one night about what we would name our kids."

"What name did you choose for your first daughter?" Ellie asked.

Angie sighed. "Genevieve Virginia Elizabeth Williams. Genevieve was Josh's mother's name, Virginia, after Nana, and of course, Elizabeth, for mom." Angie smiled. "We're going to call our daughter, Gigi, for short."

"I like it. It's perfect." Courtney sat on the floor next to her oldest sister and Euclid plopped down in between them, his huge plume of a tail swishing over Angie's lap.

"So." Ellie looked at Angie with a serious expression. "We need to keep you alive. I have every intention of meeting Gigi one day."

As Angie blinked away the moisture in her eyes and gave Ellie a nod, her hands balled into fists. She was determined to one day bring that little child into the world and hold her in her arms.

ELLIE DECIDED to do some paperwork before going to bed and the others agreed it was time to go home. Courtney and Angie were staying in one of the carriage house apartments at the rear of the Victorian while the third floor renovations were going on so they headed for the back door.

"We're taking Euclid and Circe to our apartment," Courtney informed Ellie.

Before Tom and Jenna went home, they offered to walk Mr. Finch to his house behind the Victorian. As Tom, Jenna, and Finch started along the stone walkway that connected Finch's property to the mansion, Tom said to Angie and Courtney, "Be sure and lock the doors to the apartment. Don't take any chances. You're only several yards from the Victorian and two houses away from us, but you need to be careful. Lock those doors. Tomorrow, I'll be working here on the renovations. I'm going to keep an eye on Lance. Keep the cats with you. Call us if you need anything."

After wishing the others goodnight, Angie and Courtney and the felines, climbed the stairs to the carriage house's two-bedroom apartment.

"I wish Tom wouldn't go on and on about your safety," Courtney teased Angie. "It makes me want to get away from you and share Ellie's room with her instead."

Angie made a face and Euclid hissed at Courtney.

"Sheesh, Euclid, I'm only kidding around. I wouldn't leave Angie alone."

The orange boy flicked his tail and walked away from Courtney with his nose in the air.

"He can't take a joke anymore," Courtney whispered to her sister.

Angie shrugged. "He's always been sensitive to any talk about us being in danger."

Courtney plugged in the lights for the little tree she and her sister had put up in the living room of the apartment. Euclid sniffed one of the lower branches and chewed on it for a few seconds.

"He still hopes it will turn into a real tree instead of being an artificial one." Courtney grinned.

"We'll get the real tree for the Victorian soon." Angie smiled. "Then he can climb up and hide in the branches."

"We need to remember to shore up the tree. Last year, we forgot, and the whole thing crashed to the floor when he jumped onto the branch."

"At least, we hadn't decorated it yet." Angie went to her bedroom and changed into pajamas. Courtney did the same and then she made tea for herself and her sister, and then the two settled comfortably on the sofa, along with the cats, with the intention to read for a while ... but, instead, the four of them fell sound asleep.

An hour passed and Angie woke to a soft, black paw gently poking her nose. With her eyes still closed, the young woman brushed at the tickling sensation and realized that it was Circe standing on her chest trying to wake her.

"What is it, little one?" Angie sat up rubbing her eyes and saw Courtney napping at the other end of the sofa with her mouth hanging open. She moved the cat to the side, swung her feet to the floor, and yawned before standing up.

Circe jumped down and darted to the windowsill. Looking back at Angie, she growled low in her throat and the sound of it sent a shiver down the honey-blonde's back.

"What's wrong?" Angie turned off the light so no one would see her moving around in the apartment and stepped slowly to the window, her heart racing.

Pushing the shade slightly to the side, she peeked out.

A man stood in the shadow of the huge tree. He would have been easy to miss, but Angie noticed a glint of light shining off the snaps on the man's jacket from the security light mounted on the side of the carriage house.

Angie's heart leapt into her throat as Circe let out a growl. Trying to steady her nerves by taking in long breaths, Angie forced herself to look again in the man's direction. She could see the edge of his boot and the side of his puffy ski jacket, but his face was completely hidden in the shadow.

Her mind racing, Angie thought about what she should do. Call Chief Martin? Call Tom? Her phone was on the kitchen table. If she moved to go get it, she might miss the man walking away. "Courtney," she whispered.

Her sister stirred, but didn't wake up.

Euclid lifted his head, stood up, stretched, and

jumped down to see why Angie and Circe were at the window. He leapt up onto the side table and pushed his face around the edge of the shade. Spotting the man by the tree, the Maine Coon let out a howl.

Angie stepped back from the window as Courtney sat up, blinking. "What's going on?"

"Someone's in the yard," Angie whispered. "Text Chief Martin."

Courtney grabbed her phone and sent the text. "I'll text Tom, too. Could it be a B and B guest out walking around because he couldn't sleep?"

"He's standing in the shadows, staring up at our windows," Angie said softly, still pressed against the wall.

"Let's confront him," Courtney suggested.

"I don't think that's a good idea."

"Let's draw him out. He might run off before Tom or Chief Martin can get here." Courtney strode to the window pulled the shade up and opened the window. "Who's down there?" she demanded. "What are you doing? Step into the light where I can see you."

The figure wheeled and took off towards Mr. Finch's house.

"If you ever come back here, I'll shoot you," Courtney screamed at the retreating man.

Tom dashed into the yard from the driveway wearing his pajamas and a sweater and looked up to the window. "What happened? Where did he go?"

Courtney leaned out and pointed.

"You threatened to shoot the guy," Angie said. "You don't own a gun."

"The idiot doesn't know that." Courtney ran to the bedroom to look out that window to try and see where Tom had gone.

Angie grabbed her phone and her wallet. "Come outside with me. Chief Martin will be here soon and I want to be able to hear Tom if he calls out."

When the two sisters and the cats went down the stairs and opened the door to the yard, the chief hustled from the driveway towards the carriage house with his gun drawn.

"He ran off," Angie told the chief. "He was standing under the Beech tree."

"Tom chased after him into Mr. Finch's yard," Courtney reported.

The chief took off down the walkway towards Finch's place. "Go inside. Lock the doors."

As the young women headed to go back up to the apartment, something caught Angie's eye. Euclid and Circe stood under the big tree sniffing at something on the snow where the man had been standing.

"What's there?" Angie asked and walked to see what the cats had found. Bending down, she picked up the thing, turned around, and held it up for her sister to see.

The security lamp's light glinted off what Angie had in her hand.

Courtney stepped forward. "A key?"

10

T he fire in the backyard fire pit blazed while the tiki torches set around the periphery of the garden glowed and sparkled. Ellie made s'mores for the guests and Mr. Finch and Angie handled the drink table pouring hot toddies, wine, hot cocoa, and tea.

A table with beef sliders, shrimp, mini quiches, and mushroom turnovers was set under the pergola. Urns and pots, set on the patio and near the pergola, contained white birch branches, various greens, pinecones, and slender red branches. Holiday songs played over the speakers hung near the back door of the Victorian.

Inside the house, Euclid and Circe sat on the back of the sofa in the family room watching the evening activities through the window.

"After last night, are you sure you want to be helping with this event, Miss Angie?" Finch was bundled up in a wool coat, red and green plaid scarf, and a faux fur hat pulled down over his ears.

"It's better to keep busy." Angie smiled as she handed a hot toddy to one of the guests.

People staying at the inn mingled and chatted and enjoyed the drinks and food.

The man standing under the tree near the carriage house the previous evening got away without being seen despite the efforts of Tom and Chief Martin. Tom had raced along the stone path towards Mr. Finch's house, but there was no sign of the man. The path was clear of any snow and showed no footprints so Tom had no idea if the man ran into Finch's yard or took off down the street in front of the older man's house.

Chief Martin arrived a few minutes after Tom and the two searched around the bushes and trees looking for anything to indicate which way the lurker had run. Frustrated and angry, Tom let out a few curses and Chief Martin joined in with one or two swear words. Angie showed them the key Circe had found under the tree and the chief took it to store at the station to dust for prints.

"It's a key to the Victorian," Angie told the chief. "It's the master key to all the guest rooms."

Chief Martin said, "I doubt the man would be careless enough to leave his fingerprints on the key, but I'll have it checked out nonetheless."

Angie poured black tea into two mugs and handed them to a woman and her husband. "The key might not have anything to do with the lurker," she said to Mr. Finch. "It could have been in the yard for days." Trying to make light of the situation, Angie winked at the bundled up older man. "Too bad the lurker didn't drop his ID card beside the key. He could have made it easier for us."

"If only...." Finch sighed and stomped his feet to try and warm them.

"Why don't you go stand by the fire pit to warm up for a few minutes?" Angie suggested. "I can hold down the drink station."

"I think I will do that." Finch took his cane from the side of the table and headed to stand by the fire.

As soon as Angie was alone, Marvin Oates, approached the drink table with a wide grin. "Well, I see your sister has pressed you into service."

Angie turned to see the B and B guest she'd met in the foyer of the Victorian the other day. "We all help out when we can. Are you enjoying your stay in town, Mr. Oates?"

"Call me Marvin. Indeed, I am. I love the seacoast area. It's a beautiful time of year with the dusting of snow everywhere. The town is like a wonderland. May I have a glass of red wine?"

Angie poured and handed the glass to Oates.

"This is a lovely inn. I've met your sisters. All of you are a delight, so friendly and welcoming." Oates raised the glass and sipped. "Tell me about yourself."

Although Angie couldn't pinpoint what it was, something about Oates seemed off. She gave him a brief summary of how she ended up in Sweet Cove running the bake shop.

"You inherited this house?" Oates looked up at the back of the mansion. "It must cost a fortune to care for the place. You must have been intimidated by the house at first, what with the upkeep and all."

"I was more excited and pleased that my sisters and I could move here and run our businesses. It was a dream come true."

"I guess some people have all the luck." Oates chuckled, but there seemed to be an edge to his words.

"What's all the laughter over here?" When Elizabeth Winters came up on Oates right side, Angie was glad to see her.

"We're in the middle of a nice conversation," Oates said. "How are you, Ms. Winters? Enjoying your stay here at the B and B? I haven't run into you very often."

Ms. Winters looked at Angie and ordered a hot toddy. "Maybe I'm avoiding you," she told Oates.

Oates expression turned serious for a moment and then he shook himself and laughed. "Then you'd be missing out on very pleasant company."

Angie asked Ms. Winters what she'd been doing while staying in Sweet Cove.

"I've been having a wonderful time shopping and trying the restaurants." The woman took a swallow from her glass. "Such a pretty town. I've been jogging and walking by the ocean. I'm actually feeling relaxed." Ms. Winters eyed the crowd in the backyard. "Even though that Peeping Tom is still on the loose. I heard he paid a visit here last evening."

"The Peeping Tom?" Oates asked. "Here? You mean in the yard right here?"

"That's exactly what I mean."

"We don't know who he was. He seemed to be lurking. I don't think it was the Peeping Tom." Angie tried to minimize the experience. "Maybe the man had too much to drink, got disoriented, and wandered into the yard. No harm done."

"You can try to dismiss it all you want," Ms. Winters said to Angie. "There's a creep bothering some of the women in this town. No one knows what he'll do next. I'm sure people are on edge. The police need to get on the ball and find this guy."

"Maybe you should make some suggestions to the police about how they should handle the problem," Oates remarked with a slight smile.

The woman stared at Oates with a dark expression. "Does it amuse you to have people living with fear and concern for their safety? Because this is a serious situation. Perhaps, because it's the holiday season, people are trying to ignore the unpleasantness. Well, I can tell you that would be a grave mistake."

"I'm sure the police are doing all they can," Oates said adjusting the scarf around his neck.

"Thanks for the drink," Ms. Winters told Angie before moving to the fire pit to join a group of women standing by the fire eating s'mores.

"She can be very touchy," Oates pouted as he watched Elizabeth Winters chatting with some of the other guests. "I was only trying to lighten the mood. I doubt she's in any danger. She's only here for a week or two."

"It's a difficult situation," Angie said. "It makes many people upset."

"What happened here last night?" Oates narrowed his eyes and moved closer to the drink table.

"Someone was in the yard. When we spoke to him, he ran off," Angie explained.

"Huh. Strange. It wasn't a B and B guest?"

"I didn't recognize the man."

"What did he look like?" Oates asked.

"We didn't get a good look at him. He had on a ski jacket. We didn't see his face because he was standing under the big tree." Angie gestured to the huge Beech tree by the carriage house.

"Was he wearing a winter hat?"

"We couldn't see his head."

"How old would you say he was?"

"I couldn't judge," Angie said. "We didn't see him well enough."

"Did he match the description that other women have given regarding the Peeping Tom?" Oates asked.

"I don't know." Angie wanted the conversation to come to an end.

"Do you think it was the Peeping Tom? Who else would come around the back of a house and lurk there?"

"Like I said, the man might have lost his bearings and came into the yard by accident."

Oates scoffed. "Unlikely." He lowered his voice. "But I get what you're trying to do. You don't want to alarm the guests. If they knew about the man, they'd all high-tail it back home."

"The guests have been informed." Angie crossed her arms over the front of her jacket. "We would never withhold important information from people staying here at the Victorian."

"*I* didn't know about what happened." Oates seemed to be challenging Angie.

"Ellie left a notice in everyone's rooms. You must have overlooked it."

"Hmm, I guess I missed it," Oates said. He finished his wine and requested a refill. "Do you think sometimes people blow news out of proportion?"

"Do you think that's what's happening in this situation?" Angie asked.

"I have no idea. Ms. Winters doesn't seem to think the Peeping Tom is getting the attention he deserves."

"She has valid concerns," Angie said.

"Are the police sure it's a *man* lurking at people's windows?"

One of Angie's eyebrows went up. "What do you mean?"

"Couldn't it be a woman? I mean it's winter, it's cold out. People are bundled up in hats and jackets and gloves. How can the police be sure it's a *man* running around town bothering women? Has anyone actually seen this person's face?"

"I don't know." The chief never told Angie that a description of the Peeping Tom's face had been given so she was almost certain that no one had ever seen the lurker's face.

"When did all this Peeping Tom stuff start?" Oates asked.

Angie told the man the approximate date the lurker had started his menacing of the town.

"Ah." Oates turned to watch the group of people standing around the fire pit. "Wasn't that around the same time Elizabeth Winters showed up in Sweet Cove?" The man shifted his eyes to Angie. "Interesting coincidence, isn't it?"

Angie's heart skipped a beat and when she glanced to the window of the family room she could see Euclid standing behind the glass, his tail up, flicking back and forth ... his mouth wide open to release a hiss.

An icy cold finger seemed to trace down Angie's back.

Could the Peeping Tom be a woman?

11

ngie had closed the bake shop for the day and stepped out to the porch that ran along the side of the house to add some greens and berries to the pots on each side of the shop door. Out of the corner of her eye, she noticed someone sitting at the small metal café table on the porch and she turned to see Lance, the renovation worker.

Walking down to speak to him, Angie greeted the young man. "You can eat your lunch inside in the kitchen, if you want to. You don't need to sit out here in the cold."

"Thanks, but if it's okay, I like to be outside. Would you rather I didn't sit here?"

"Not at all. It's fine if you want to sit. If it gets

much colder though, please use the kitchen or the dining room in the house."

"I appreciate it." Lance bit into his sandwich. The young man didn't want to meet Angie's gaze and he hunched over his lunch in a way that made him seem like he'd prefer to disappear than have a conversation with the woman standing before him.

"How's the work going?" Angie asked.

"Good." Lance nodded as he chewed.

"Tom gave us a tour. I think the apartments are going to be great."

Lance only nodded.

"You worked in Maine before taking the job with Tom's company?"

"Yes, ma'am."

Angie almost smiled at being called ma'am. She figured she must only be a year older than Lance. "Had you lived in Maine long?"

"No." Lance didn't look up. "I like it better in Massachusetts."

"What didn't you like about living in Maine?" Angie asked.

"I didn't know anybody. I was lonely." Lance chewed faster to finish his lunch so he could get away from the questions.

The young man's reply made Angie's heart squeeze. "That's understandable. If I didn't have my family around, I'd sure be lonely. Your family lives around here?"

"I only have my grandmother ... she lives outside of Boston. I have a few friends ... they're about forty minutes away."

"That's closer than being hours away from them." Angie smiled, but Lance didn't look up. He focused on the last bite of his sandwich and then crumpled up the wrapper and stuffed it into the paper bag. "I better get back to work." The young man strode away to return to the third floor of the house.

Angie wasn't sure what to make of Lance's abruptness. Maybe he was shy or socially awkward or uncomfortable talking to the homeowner afraid she might ask something about the renovations that should be directed to Tom.

Whatever the reason, he couldn't scurry back to work fast enough.

Ronald, the other worker, stood at the back of his truck looking for a tool. He noticed Lance hurry by and then saw Angie walking along the porch to the bake shop door.

"Afternoon," Ronald called. He had the tool he needed in his hand and headed to the front of the house, but stopped to speak with Angie. "Everything okay? I saw Lance."

Angie gave a nod. "Oh, sure. Lance was eating his lunch on the porch. I told him he could sit in the kitchen where it was warmer. You're welcome to have your lunch there, too."

"Thanks a lot. That's very nice of you." Ronald looked at the porch. "You don't mind if Lance eats on the porch?"

"He can certainly sit out here if he wants to."

"Lance is kind of a quiet pup. He works hard, does quality work, but he's not much of a talker. We don't shoot the breeze at all. Our communication is made up of discussion about the job we're doing. I don't mind. I feel sorry for the guy."

Angie tilted her head slightly. "Why? Because he's so shy?"

"The kid went through a trauma when he was about nine," Ronald said. "He saw his father kill his mother."

Angie let out a gasp.

"Yup. It happened right in front of him. Can you imagine that?" Ronald shook his head slowly from side to side. "After I found that out, I had a better understanding of why the kid is so quiet. Must have messed him up in a bad way."

"Did Lance tell you what happened to his mother?"

"No way. I can barely get a *yes* or a *no* from him. I was telling my wife about Lance and she looked him up on the internet. Some news stories came up about it, not a lot of information since it happened about twenty years ago, but the story was there."

"What's Lance's last name?"

"McCullough. How could you ever be right in the head after that?" Ronald said, "His mom had a restraining order against the guy. Guess that didn't work out for her, huh? If you want anything or have questions about the upstairs reno, it might be better to ask me than to talk to Lance. People make him uncomfortable."

"Does Tom know about Lance's mother?"

Ronald gave a shrug. "Not from me. I try to stay out of folks' business. I only told you because you were trying to talk to Lance. I wouldn't spread it around none. Wouldn't do the kid any good to have people talking about him."

Angie nodded. "Thanks for letting me know. I don't want to cause him any distress."

THE ROSELAND SISTERS and Mr. Finch prepared a simple dinner of beef burgers and veggie burgers, grilled asparagus, and rice so they'd be ready when Tom and Josh arrived to head to the Christmas tree farm. The cats rested on top of the refrigerator watching the family members bustle around.

Angie told the family about what she'd learned about Lance and what Marvin Oates said the previous evening about Elizabeth Winters arriving in town around the same time the Peeping Tom began his antics.

Ellie frowned. "A *woman* might be the Peeping Tom? That was not in my head at all. Is it possible?"

"I suppose anything is possible." Courtney removed the burgers from the broiling pan and placed them on platters. "Maybe we need to keep an eye on Ms. Winters."

Jenna scooped the rice from the sauce pot into a serving bowl. "It sounds to me like Marvin Oates doesn't like Elizabeth Winters and might enjoy spreading rumors about her."

"I've seen the two of them engaged in minor disagreements," Finch said. "They both seem to have strong opinions and don't mind expressing them. It can lead to some friction. I get the impression that Mr. Oates prefers a woman to keep her thoughts to herself."

Courtney snorted. "Then he's staying in the wrong house if he doesn't like opinionated women."

The back door opened and Tom came into the kitchen. "I like opinionated women. The stronger, the better." He gave Jenna a hug and a kiss. "A man who doesn't appreciate strength of mind and purpose in others isn't confidant in himself."

Tom took some plates from the cabinets and went to help Mr. Finch set the kitchen table for dinner. "I was able to leave a construction project early today, so I can have dinner with all of you. What were you discussing when I came in?"

Finch told Tom about Marvin Oates and Elizabeth Winters.

Tom gave a chuckle. "Just because someone shows up in Sweet Cove around the time of a crime, that arrival doesn't mean the person is involved in the wrongdoing. Mr. Oates seems to be enjoying spreading rumors."

Angie brought up Lance. "I learned something about one of your workers today."

Tom's face became serious as he listened to his sister-in-law explain what Ronald had told her about Lance. "Well, heck. I did not know anything about that. The poor guy. What a horrible thing to have happened."

"He isn't much younger than us," Angie said. "But most of us feel like he's just a kid. His manner and his avoidance of conversation make him seem much younger than he is."

When the group sat down to eat, Courtney spoke. "I hate to bring this up because I feel really badly about what Lance has been through."

All eyes turned to the youngest Roseland.

Courtney said, "Sometimes, people who have suffered trauma like Lance, end up turning to crime."

Finch gave a curt nod. "It's true. The trauma deeply damages them. Some become abusive in their relationships, some become abusive to themselves, and sometimes, the person engages in criminal activity."

Angie's face blanched. "You mean Lance might be the Peeping Tom?"

"It's possible," Courtney said, "but we can't jump to conclusions. The guy is most likely completely innocent. It wouldn't hurt to keep an eye on him though."

"You should probably share this information with Chief Martin," Ellie said to her sister.

"I'll tell him." Angie looked sad. "I hate to be suspicious of someone who hasn't done anything wrong."

Ellie said, "Yet. The other thing to remember is Lance had that newspaper clipping about Angie tucked in his toolbox."

"There's probably a simple explanation for that." Angie hoped so anyway.

"It's important to be cautious," Tom said. "You can still be kind to the guy, just don't put your head in the sand ... especially now. You've had some recent warnings about your safety being compromised. It's important to keep our eyes and ears open and be aware and careful." Tom's face softened and he smiled at Angie. "So. Gigi, huh? It's a pretty name."

Angie blushed.

"I'm looking forward to meeting that little daughter of yours one day," Tom said.

"But before we can meet her, we need to keep Angie safe." Jenna reached over and squeezed her sister's hand.

"And," Finch cleared his throat, "we must remember that it might not be the Peeping Tom who means to do Miss Angie harm. Danger may come from a different direction."

Euclid let out a hiss and Angie's blood turned to ice.

12

———

Standing under the lights of the Christmas tree farm, the cold night air made Angie's cheeks turn rosy red as Josh handed her a cup of hot cocoa with whipped cream on top. When Josh pretended to clink her paper mug with his own cup of cocoa, Angie laughed, and the two took careful sips of the steaming liquid.

Evergreens of all sizes and shapes stood in rows leaning against the wooden rails that kept them upright. Couples and families strolled along the aisles of Blue Spruces, Douglas Firs, Norway Spruces, and other varieties searching for the perfect tree. The scent of the evergreens floated on the air. A bonfire blazed off to the side and people stood close to it to warm their hands while listening to a band play on a stage set up away from the bonfire.

Mr. Finch and his girlfriend, Betty, a Sweet Cove Realtor, walked slowly hand in hand admiring the many beautiful trees. "I would like a small one," Finch told Betty. "Nothing towering or imposing. Something simple, elegant."

"This is a lovely one, Victor," Betty pointed out a small, symmetrical tree with deep green needles.

Ellie and Jack hunted for two trees, one for Jack's office and one for the living room of his Cape-style house. Courtney and Rufus had been charged with finding a tall, full tree for the Victorian's foyer and a round, full evergreen to place in the living room.

Tom and Jenna weren't sure what kind of tree they wanted so the two wandered the aisles checking for just the right one.

"What is our task?" Josh asked Angie.

"We're looking for a tree for the family room and a big wreath for the front door." Angie slipped her hand through Josh's arm. "It's so pretty out, the trees, the snow, the bonfire."

Josh leaned down and kissed his fiancée. "We really need to set a wedding date. We need to start our life together."

Angie beamed up at the handsome man. "Which season should we choose?"

"Spring," Josh said. "Because that's when I first met you."

After an hour of looking at trees and finally making their selections, some of the evergreens were loaded into Tom's pickup truck while the others were marked with "Sold" tags and would be held until the next afternoon when Tom would return for them.

"We thought it would be fun to go over to the bonfire for a little while," Courtney told the group. "Then we can go home and decorate the tree we set up in the foyer."

The family and friends walked over to warm themselves by the fire and listen to the bluegrass band. When the band started the third song, Jenna hustled over to her twin sister.

"I think we should leave now." Jenna's eyes moved about the crowd and she stood tall and stiff.

"What's wrong?" Angie asked as a sputter of nervousness pinged at her.

"Nothing. I just think it's time to go."

"It seems sudden." Angie pushed for information. "We've been by the fire only a little while."

Josh made eye contact with Jenna. "Why do you think it's time we left?"

"I feel uneasy," Jenna admitted. "It's probably foolishness, but I don't think we should be here."

Josh took hold of Angie's arm. "You don't have to tell me twice. I don't care if it's a false alarm or not, I think we should head home right now."

Mr. Finch came up to them holding tight to his cane and being careful not to slip on any ice or hard snow. He gave Jenna a look.

"I told them I feel uneasy," Jenna said.

Finch nodded and forced a smile. "Why don't we go home now and decorate the tree while we have some nice, hot tea. Enough cold weather for me this evening."

"You sense something, Mr. Finch?" Angie's voice was tinged with worry.

"I sense it would be more pleasant at home," Finch said. "Why don't you two head off and I'll go collect Miss Betty and tell the others we're leaving. See you at the house."

Jenna sent Tom a text.

"You don't have to stand here with me," Angie said. "You can go get Tom."

"I'm staying right here beside you. Fuss if you

like, but I am maintaining my position." Jenna gave Angie a poke with her elbow.

Tom hurried over. "I'll walk with you to Josh's car and then I'll get the truck and meet you at the Victorian."

Walking through the Christmas tree farm on the way to the parking area, a voice called to them. "It's the Roselands. Two of them, anyway."

"Ms. Winters," Jenna said. "Enjoying the evening?"

"I am. This is a perfect winter night." Elizabeth Winters was dressed in a bulky, dark blue parka with a fur-trimmed hood. A wool winter cap was pulled down over her ears. "I came to hear the bluegrass band."

"We listened for a while," Angie said. "They're very good."

"Now we have to get home." Jenna tugged at Angie's sleeve. "Have a nice time."

"Okay, thanks." Ms. Winters seemed surprised by their need to hurry off, but she gave a nod and a wave and started for the bonfire.

"Is it really necessary to dash off like this?" Angie asked.

"Yes." Jenna took her sister's arm and dragged her to Josh's car.

ON ARRIVING HOME, Jenna led the way down the hall. "Let's go sit in the family room."

"Why?" Angie's eyes narrowed.

"Mr. Finch wants me to look through his sketchbook. We both felt I had to do it."

"Is that why we had to run like scared rabbits from the bonfire?"

"Yes." Jenna sank onto the sofa as the cats came into the room and jumped up to sit next to the sisters. "I also felt unsafe there."

"Like paranormal feelings or normal worry feelings?" Angie ran her hand over Circe's smooth fur.

"Both. Mr. Finch also sensed it would be better for us to leave."

Mr. Finch and Josh came into the room carrying cups of tea for all of them.

"Miss Betty is in the sunroom," Finch said. "She has some calls to return for her business so we have some time for Jenna to look at the new sketches."

Josh sat next to Angie and took her hand.

"Okay, let's do it." Jenna reached to take the sketchbook from Finch's hand and she set it on her lap.

"The newest drawings begin where the sticky tab

is attached to the page," Finch gestured. He nervously pushed his glasses up the bridge of his nose as Jenna began to study the new sketches.

Angie could see beads of perspiration begin to form on her sister's forehead.

Jenna stopped at one of the pictures and stared, her eyes seeming to glaze over.

Angie was about to speak when Finch caught her eye and shook his head, so instead, she slid closer to Jenna to see what was drawn on the page.

A gasp caught in Angie's throat. Finch had drawn the Christmas tree farm.

Jenna moved a shaky finger over the lines and shadings that Finch had created. The aisles of trees, the white lights strung overhead, the bonfire, the band playing, people standing in groups or choosing a tree.

Jenna moved her finger over the large group of people standing in front of the stage listening to the music. Her eyes closed and she leaned slightly forward ... then her eyes popped open and she sat straight, her chest heaving as she tried to catch her breath.

"What is it? Did you see something?" Angie placed her hand gently on Jenna's arm.

"Yes." Jenna looked at Mr. Finch.

"What was it, Miss Jenna?"

"A woman. Near the stage." Jenna put her hands on the sides of her head and a few tears dropped onto the sketchbook in her lap. "Something happened ... to the woman."

"Do you know who she is?" Angie asked as Josh tightened his grip on her hand.

"No ... maybe. I don't know. I'm not sure."

Angie looked closely at the drawing, but couldn't see anything in the picture except people with smiling faces by the bandstand. "Did you see the same ring of fire you've seen in other drawings Mr. Finch has done?"

"Yes. The ring of fire was right in front of the stage." Jenna touched the spot in the sketch where she'd seen it. "The woman was within the ring. Then it all disappeared."

"What does it mean?" Angie asked.

"It means someone got injured at the Christmas tree farm tonight." Jenna closed the sketchbook and handed it back to Mr. Finch. She brushed the dots of perspiration from her skin and leaned back against the sofa.

Tom stood behind the couch and tenderly rubbed his wife's shoulders.

Euclid gave the young woman a lick on her hand

and Jenna scooped the big orange cat into her arms and rested her cheek on his fluffy fur.

Courtney, still wearing her winter jacket, flew into the room, her eyes wide, and when she saw the family gathered around Jenna, she stopped in her tracks. "Are you okay?"

Jenna gave a weak nod.

"Did you see something in Mr. Finch's sketches?" Courtney asked, her voice breathless.

Jenna nodded. Her muscles felt like rubber. She could barely move.

"Was the Christmas tree farm in the sketches?"

All eyes in the room stared at Courtney.

"Jenna saw a woman at the farm," Angie said. "She thinks something happened to the woman."

"Well, Jenna's right. The woman's dead. Someone stabbed her."

Jenna covered her eyes with her hand.

"Who was it?" Angie jumped to her feet. "Do you know?"

"Chief Martin showed up with some other police officers," Courtney said. "He saw me in the crowd and came over. He asked me to tell you that the woman's name was Bella Masters. He said you and Jenna had talked to her about the Peeping Tom."

Angie's mouth dropped open.

Bella Masters was the woman who had pulled a gun on the Peeping Tom when he showed up at her back door one night. Now she was dead.

13

Before the sun was up, Chief Martin sat with the Roselands, Mr. Finch, Josh, and Tom in the Victorian's family room to report on the incident from the prior evening. The chief looked like he hadn't slept at all, his eyelids drooped and stubble showed on his chin and cheeks.

"I managed to go home, shower, and grab some toast after leaving the station an hour ago. We were at the Christmas tree farm until the wee hours. Heck of a thing." He shook his head.

Ellie stood and headed for the kitchen. "I'll get you some eggs and hot coffee."

The chief looked grateful.

"We left the farm shortly before the attack took place," Jenna informed the chief.

"We both had a sensation of danger and were afraid it might be targeted towards Miss Angie," Finch explained. "So we decided it would be best to leave the farm and return home."

"Can you tell us what happened?" Courtney asked. Listening intently, Euclid sat in the young woman's lap with his back feet hanging over the edge of the chair.

Chief Martin ran his hand over his face. "Bella Masters had arrived about thirty minutes prior to the incident and was planning to meet two friends there to listen to the band. She stood off to the side, near the back, so it would be easier for her friends to spot her in the crowd. The band was about halfway through the set. Someone came up behind Ms. Masters and cut her throat."

Angie stifled a gasp. "Was the attacker seen by anyone?"

"Everyone was focused on the band," the chief told them. "Ms. Masters fell to the ground and two people next to her went to her aid thinking the woman had fainted. They tried to stop the flow of blood, but...."

"So they didn't see the person who attacked her," Courtney said.

"They did not."

"Did anyone notice anything that seemed off?" Jenna asked. "Someone acting suspicious? Someone running away? Anything?"

"We talked to the people who were present and no one saw a thing."

"No one?" Courtney's eyes flashed. "How can that be? People were around the woman. She gets murdered in a crowd and not one single person saw what happened?"

The chief took in a deep breath. "It's cold outside, people are bundled up. It would be easy to conceal a knife in the sleeve of a winter jacket. Slip it down to the hand when the person approached the victim, come up from behind, put an arm around the woman and with the other hand, make the cut. Anyone glancing around might think the person was being affectionate, coming up from behind and hugging the woman. Everyone's attention was on the band."

Jenna gave a nod of understanding. "And when the woman fell, people would be focused on going to her aid, thinking she was ill and had fainted, no one would be looking around for an attacker."

"Do you think this attack is related to the Peeping Tom?" Angie asked.

"It could be. We aren't dismissing the possibility.

As you all know, Bella had two visits from the Peeping Tom, two nights in a row."

"He didn't go back to her house again?" Courtney asked. "It was only the two times?"

Chief Martin said, "It was only two times that Bella saw him."

"It doesn't make a lot of sense though." Angie moved a little to the side of the sofa when Circe jumped up to sit between her and Josh. "Why choose a public place to kill Ms. Masters? If it was the Peeping Tom who did this, why not just break into the woman's house at night and attack her? There would be much less chance of being seen and caught than doing this in public with so many people around."

Ellie returned to the room with a tray for the chief holding a plate heaped with scrambled eggs, two pancakes, bacon, and an English muffin with butter and jam along with a large mug of steaming, black coffee.

With an appreciative smile, Chief Martin accepted the plate of food and the cup of coffee with thanks.

"Dig in," Ellie said. "We need you healthy and strong."

Chief Martin eagerly lifted a forkful of eggs to

his mouth and then addressed Angie's question about why the Peeping Tom might choose a public place to kill Ms. Masters rather than at the woman's home. "Sometimes, perpetrators get cocky and arrogant and mock the police by boldly committing a crime. It's a way of thumbing his or her nose at law enforcement. It's a statement along the lines of – *see what I can do and you can't catch me.*"

"It's a power trip," Josh said.

"Exactly," the chief gave a nod.

"If someone is becoming so bold," Tom speculated, "it must mean more danger for the town."

"It can, yes," the chief said.

"But it might not be the Peeping Tom who killed Bella Masters," Ellie pointed out. "It could be completely unrelated. It could be someone else who did this."

"Do you know Ms. Master's background?" Angie asked. "Enemies? Problems? An angry ex-husband? Anything that could point to someone she knew?"

"We're looking into that right now. I'll let you know if we find anything of concern. We know that she held a Ph.D. in physics and taught science at the community college in Salem. She'd been in the news recently. Ms. Masters, or I should say, Dr. Masters, was calling for the financial head of the school to step down due to mismanagement of funds."

"So she could have made enemies over that," Ellie said.

"Yes," the chief said. "Dr. Masters was also an elected member of the Sweet Cove town finance committee."

"Another place she might have made some enemies," Angie guessed.

The chief took a long swallow of his coffee and then sighed. "I needed that." The stocky man looked to Jenna and Finch. "That's about all I can tell you of what happened last evening. Can you tell me what you picked up on last night that caused you to leave the farm?"

Jenna said, "We'd been at the farm for about an hour and a half. We were all walking around picking out trees. The band was playing and we were cold so we headed over to the bonfire. I started to feel uneasy, worried, like something was wrong or was about to be wrong." The young woman made eye contact with Finch. "Mr. Finch came to speak with me. He said he felt anxious, something was making him feel we should head home, that it was important for us to leave the farm. When I heard that, I went straight to Angie and told her we had to leave."

"Was the worry intangible?" the chief asked, "or did it feel like it was associated with the Peeping Tom?"

"It was an unfocused worry," Finch said. "It was like a premonition of danger, but what the cause of the danger would be, we couldn't pinpoint it."

"We thought we shouldn't take any chances so we headed home." Jenna squeezed Tom's hand, thankful for his steady presence.

Finch continued the story, "When we arrived home, we sat together and I gave my sketchbook to Miss Jenna to look through. Earlier, I had a burst of creative output and made several drawings. I had the feeling one of them might reveal something."

"And it did?" the chief asked.

Jenna nodded. "Mr. Finch had drawn the Christmas tree farm, the bonfire, and the stage where the band was playing. There was a crowd in front of the stage." After pausing for a few moments, she continued, "When I'm about to get an image from one of Mr. Finch's drawings, my vision starts to dim and then I see a small circle outlined in fire. In the center of the circle, I see something that isn't drawn in the sketch, but is related to the picture. Last night, I saw a woman in distress."

"Could you see the people around her?" the chief questioned.

"Only in shadow, nothing in detail," Jenna reported.

"Did you know she'd been stabbed?"

"No. I only felt fear and distress."

"Could you see who the woman was?" the chief asked. "Did you know it was Bella Masters?"

Jenna sighed. "No. I only felt the sensations."

"When we heard what Jenna had seen and felt," Finch said, "we were thankful we had left the farm when we did."

Angie's mind raced. "Have there been recent incidents of the Peeping Tom?"

"It's been quiet for a few days," Chief Martin said. "We haven't had any reports for three days."

"So if the Peeping Tom killed Bella Masters, was he saving his energy for the attack? Was he busy planning the attack over the past few days so he didn't venture out to stand outside people's windows?" Angie asked. "What would that mean? Will he try to attack others now? Will he return to looking in windows or will he abandon that activity?"

"We really have no idea how he will proceed," the chief said. "My advice, as always, is to be aware and alert. Stay with others, avoid going anywhere alone at night. Keep your phones at the ready."

"Did you look into what I learned about Tom's employee, Lance McCullough?" Angie asked. "Is it true he saw his mother killed?"

"It's true." The chief nodded. "He has a clean record ... no record of arrests or misdemeanors. His former employer said the young man is a skilled, hard worker, although extremely quiet and seems unsocial."

"That describes Lance," Tom said. "He's a talented carpenter and woodworker."

"Does he live in Sweet Cove?" Courtney asked.

"He rents a small place over near Silver Cove. He moved there right after Tom hired him."

"When did you hire him?" Finch asked.

Tom made a face. "Shortly before the Peeping Tom stuff started."

A chill ran over Angie's skin.

14

Ellie put the platter of oatmeal-butterscotch cookies on the living room coffee table next to the silver pot of hot cocoa. As holiday music played and a fire blazed in the fireplace, Angie pulled red ribbons, small silver bells, white angels, and colorful glass ornaments from the boxes scattered over the floor.

Courtney, Jenna, and Mr. Finch carefully placed each ornament on the branches of the tree under the watchful supervision of Euclid and Circe.

"I guess Euclid thinks we're doing a good job because he just closed his eyes," Courtney chuckled.

Everyone looked to see the big orange cat snoozing away, curled up on the rug in front of the fireplace. Circe rested next to the fluffy feline, but had her eyes on the family's activities.

"Your partner fell asleep so it's all up to you now, Circe, to make sure we do a good job on the tree." Jenna winked at the cat.

The sweet black cat trilled at the young woman and then started to purr.

"She takes her duties seriously," Finch said with a smile.

Josh, Tom, Jack, and Rufus, and Betty would arrive later to see the trees and have dessert with the family. When the living room tree was decorated, the family sat around the fire to admire their work.

"That's the last one," Courtney looked over the ornaments and red ribbons. "This one is my favorite, although I do love the family room tree, too."

"Each one is special in its own way," Jenna said. "The foyer tree is so tall and grand and the smaller one in the dining room looks great with the dried cranberries and candles. I love them all."

"And tomorrow, you'll love the one we help you and Tom put up in your house," Finch said and then chuckled. "I think we have Christmas overload going on."

"Not for me." Courtney moved to sit on the floor near the cats in front of the fire. "I love everything about the holidays. It can never be overload for me."

The front door opened and Elizabeth Winters

stepped into the foyer and brushed a little snow from the shoulders of her wool coat. When she noticed the family sitting in the living room, she said, "Well, it certainly looks festive in here. The trees are beautiful."

Ellie stood up to greet the guest. "We've put out tea, coffee, hot cocoa, wine, and some desserts on the buffet table in the dining room. Help yourself. You're welcome to join us in here by the fire."

"Thanks, but I'm going upstairs to my room for a shower and then I'm going out to the resort for a late dinner." Elizabeth headed for the staircase to go to her room. "The house looks great," she said before disappearing to the second floor.

Angie had hoped the woman would sit with them for a while. She wanted to ask her if she was near the bandstand when Bella Masters was attacked.

"I've been thinking," Courtney began. "You know how Mr. Oates suggested to Angie that the Peeping Tom could be a woman? What are your thoughts on that?"

"I didn't consider that a possibility until Oates brought it up," Angie said. "It *could* be a woman, I suppose."

"Oates implied the Peeping Tom might be Elizabeth Winters," Courtney reminded the group, keeping her voice down. "Ms. Winters arrived at the Christmas tree farm shortly before Bella was killed." Her eyes moved from person to person.

Angie's eyes went wide. "That's right, she did."

Jenna said, "And she arrived in the area around the same time the peeping started."

"Could Ms. Winters have some sort of vendetta against the residents of Sweet Cove?" Ellie asked. "Could she have known Bella Masters? Maybe she had a run-in of some sort with Bella?"

"It would be interesting to look into that." Finch tapped his chin with his index finger. "Find out if the two women knew each other."

"The killer could be living here under our roof," Courtney said with a shudder.

Finch said, "This is speculation only, but if Ms. Winters knew Bella Masters and there was bad blood between them, perhaps Ms. Winters planned to throw off the police by acting the part of a Peeping Tom ... have law enforcement suspecting there was a man in town spying in women's windows. In reality, her real intent could have been killing Bella and deflecting suspicion onto the supposed Peeping Tom."

"Wow," Jenna said. "What a clever scheme that

would be ... making the town think there was a Peeping Tom around when it was really her pretending to be an intruder."

"I suppose anyone could fit that profile." Courtney scratched under Circe's chin. "The real target might have been Bella. Whoever killed her might have done what Mr. Finch suggested, go around acting like a Peeping Tom in order to confuse police."

"Do you think someone who planned that sort of thing would pick such a public space to actually kill Bella?" Jenna asked. "If the person went to such pains to create a Peeping Tom, why attack the woman in a crowd? Wouldn't the killer attack Bella in her home? Why take a chance at being caught after spending time making up a Peeping Tom? It doesn't seem to fit the profile."

"That's true," Finch said. "If it is a real Peeping Tom who has been sneaking around people's back-yards, then the escalation of killing Bella in public makes more sense. The Peeper is doing what Chief Martin mentioned ... showing his power by not getting caught no matter what he does or where he does it."

"I agree," Ellie nodded. "If someone spent time creating a fake Peeping Tom to throw off the police, he or she wouldn't take the chance of being caught by killing Bella in public. It seems like two different mindsets, two different kinds of criminals."

"So are we eliminating Elizabeth Winters?" Angie asked.

Jenna frowned, glanced into the foyer, and said softly, "I don't think so. Ms. Winters might be crazy. She might actually be a Peeping Tom. She might be the one who killed Bella. I know there isn't any real evidence pointing to her, but there isn't any real evidence pointing at anyone. And she *was* at the bandstand last night. Elizabeth Winters is staying on my suspect list."

"Let's look her up," Courtney suggested. "Let's see what the internet says about her."

Jenna went to get her laptop. "Where did she say she works?"

Angie told her sister what Elizabeth had reported about where she worked. "She said she was a vice president there."

Jenna tapped on the keyboard. "Here's their website. She's on there as a vice president. Her bio says she graduated from the University of Chicago and got her MBA from the Wharton school at the University of Pennsylvania. She's worked at this financial firm for ten years."

Angie looked over her sister's shoulder. "She and Bella Masters are about the same age."

"We should look up Bella and see what's out there about her," Courtney said. "Chief Martin said she worked at the community college in Salem."

Jenna's fingers flew over the keys of the laptop. "Here she is on the college's website." Jenna summarized. "Bella won a teaching award three years in a row, she was committed to the idea of community college bettering students' lives and propelling them into careers, she was a favorite of the students."

"Where did she study?" Ellie asked.

"Let's see ... she received her Ph.D. from MIT." Jenna's eyes widened. "She got a bachelor's degree from the University of Chicago."

"Bella and Elizabeth Winters were both graduates of Chicago?" Angie's heart raced. "They're about the same age. Could they have known each other as undergraduates?"

"Could Elizabeth have carried a grudge against Bella for over thirty years?" Mr. Finch asked.

Courtney's face was serious. "If Elizabeth Winters is responsible for this mess...." She let her voice trail off. "And if she tries to hurt Angie...." The youngest Roseland balled her hands into fists.

"We don't have any evidence to suggest the two

women knew each other," Ellie cautioned. "Let's not get ahead of ourselves. We're only discussing possibilities and scenarios. Let's talk to Chief Martin and keep our eyes on Elizabeth."

"We also need to remember that Lance, the carpenter, arrived in town around the same time as the Peeping Tom began his rounds," Jenna said. "He suffered a severe trauma as a child and is unsocial. I wonder where he was last night around the time that Bella was attacked."

"That's a good question," Angie admitted. "There have to be more possible suspects than Elizabeth and Lance. The chief mentioned he wanted us to talk with more of the people who had the Peeping Tom in their yards. Maybe someone will recall an important detail about the person."

"We can hope," Jenna said.

"And what about the people at the bandstand last night?" Courtney asked. "The chief might want us to talk to some of the people who were listening to the band. Someone may have seen something." Courtney's expression brightened. "Maybe we should go back to the farm and walk around. Maybe we can pick up on something about the killer."

"Why don't we do that soon," Angie said. "Let's

ask the chief if it would be okay for us to walk around the bandstand area."

"There's someone out there who knows something that will help solve the case," Finch said.

"We just have to find them," Angie said trying to be hopeful.

Finch raised an eyebrow. "I also think I should shake hands with two certain people, or perhaps, hold something they are holding. I might learn a thing or two about them." Finch was sometimes able to sense things about a person if he held their hand or held an object at the same time the person had hold of it.

A smile spread over Angie's face. "Now, why didn't we think of that earlier?"

15

Small paper cups with samples of gingerbread latte and peppermint hot chocolate stood at the end of the counter in the bake shop along with mini slices of cranberry and white chocolate cake nestled in little paper and tin foil holders for the customers to try.

The shop was abuzz with customers coming in and leaving with their orders or staying to sit at the tables to chat with friends and acquaintances.

Of course, the prevailing topic of conversation was the murder of Bella Masters and the Peeping Tom with customers discussing their opinions on how to catch the criminal and who it might be.

Angie and her employee, Louisa, worked the counter, carried drinks and sweets to customers, and cleared and wiped down the tables, pausing occasionally to answer someone's question or to say a few words about the town news.

The bell tinkled above the door and Angie glanced up to see Lance coming into the bake shop. He looked around shyly, put his hands into his jacket pockets, and joined the short line at the counter. When it was his turn, Angie greeted the young man with a warm smile. "Good morning, what can I get you?"

"A large coffee with milk and one sugar, please." Lance made eye contact with Angie for only a moment before shifting his gaze to the counter.

When Angie went to make the drink, Mr. Finch came into the shop through the door that connected Angie's café to the main house. "I'm on my way to the candy store. Miss Courtney called and said the place is swamped with customers so I'm going in early. Just wanted you to know where I was in case you need me."

Angie gave Finch's arm an affectionate squeeze. "It seems it's a busy day everywhere today." The young woman leaned close to Finch and whispered. "I'm making this coffee for Lance, the carpenter. He's standing at the takeout counter." She raised an eyebrow. "Maybe I should introduce you?"

Finch understood Angie's intent. "That would be a very good idea."

Angie carried Lance's cup over to him with Finch walking beside her. "Here you go," she said and begin to ring in the sale. "This is Mr. Finch, a member of our family." To Finch, she said, "This is Lance McCullough. He's working on the third floor renovations."

When Finch greeted the man and extended his hand to shake, Lance looked at it warily, hesitated, but then went ahead and shook with the older gentleman ... with his glove on. Angie wondered if the glove would prevent Finch from sensing anything from Lance.

"The renovation looks wonderful," Finch complimented the young man. "You are a very skilled worker."

Lance gave a nervous nod, paid for the coffee, and turned away, hurrying to the exit.

"A man of few words," Finch remarked.

Angie gave him the eye. "Did you feel anything from him?"

"The handshake was brief and his hand covered in wool. I picked up what you sense when you look at him, nervousness, lack of confidence, a desire to slink away without interacting, a fear of the world."

"Any anger? Resentment? A sense of wanting to get even with the world?" Angie asked.

"No." Finch shook his head. "There was sadness, hurt, a sense of being unsure of who to trust. Other things might have been blocked by the shortness of the handshake and by the glove on his hand. I picked up on the most obvious of the young man's feelings. Just because that is all I sensed, does not mean other emotions are not there. They could be further down in the man's psyche."

"Maybe you can shake with him another day," Angie's voice was hopeful.

"I'll watch for him," Finch said. "I might drop my cane when Lance is nearby and he might pick it up and hand it to me." He gave Angie a wink. "Now, I'm off to sell candy."

Angie wished the man a good day. "See you later this evening."

Francine from the stained glass shop sat near the windows with two other women. She waved for Angie to come over. "What do you think about the woman from town being killed? Do you think it was the Peeping Tom who did it?" Francine's emerald green eyes clouded with worry.

Angie was about to speak when one of the women at the table said, "The Peeping Tom showed up one night at Francine's store. He was looking in her window. He was staring at her. It was late at night." The redhead looked at her friend with concern. "I told Francine to get a weapon."

"I got some pepper spray," Francine reported.

"I meant something better than pepper spray," the friend said. "You need to be able to defend yourself."

"I'm not getting a gun." Francine set her cup down with a clunk.

The other friend at the table said, "Bella Masters had a gun. It didn't do her any good."

"Bella didn't have it with her at the bandstand," the redhead said.

"My point, exactly," the other friend said. "It didn't do any good to have the gun."

Angie was about to head back to the counter when she heard the redhead say, "I wonder if that guy from the finance board did it. He and Bella did not get along. In fact, Troy hated Bella. He said more than once that she was a know-it-all, had terrible ideas about how to control the town's money."

"Troy is on the finance committee?" Angie asked.

"He sure is. He's a pain. Bella spoke her mind, is what I'm told. She didn't back down. I didn't know the woman though, it's just what I've heard."

"A pushy person." A man spoke behind Angie and she turned to see who it was. Marvin Oates stood there.

"Who is a pushy person?" Angie asked the man.

"The woman who got killed," Oates said.

"You knew her?" Angie narrowed her eyes.

"Of course not."

"Then why are you saying she was pushy?" Angie took a step closer and looked Oates in the eye. "Is being pushy a reason to kill someone?"

"I guess the killer thought so," Oates said with a smile.

"That's very rude." Angie's blood boiled. "And very insensitive." She stormed past the fool and headed for the counter.

"I'd like a peppermint latte," Oates called to her as he slipped into a chair by the windows.

Angie glared at Oates as she went to take orders from the several people waiting in line. "You'll have to wait. There are people ahead of you."

When the other customers had been served, Louisa made the drink for Oates and carried it to his table.

"Thanks," Angie said while wiping down the machines. "If I brought it to him, I would have dumped it over his head." She explained to Louisa what Oates had said about Bella Masters being a pushy woman.

Louisa put her hand on her hip. "If I'd known what he said, *I* would have poured the latte over his head."

Angie grinned. "I guess it's a good thing you didn't know."

Louisa adjusted her blue apron. "You know that guy who came in earlier?"

"What guy?" Angie asked.

"The slender one, he looks kind of shy."

"What about him?"

"He's cute. He seems nice." Louisa's cheeks flushed pink. "You know him?"

Angie stared at her friend and employee, but before she could answer, Ellie came into the bake shop from the house.

"Do you have any extra muffins I could take for the B and B guests?" Ellie asked. "I underestimated how many I needed this morning."

Angie took a look in the glass case. "Sure, take what you need." She reached under the counter. "Here's a box to put them in."

Ellie spotted Marvin Oates sitting at a table reading a newspaper and she kept her voice down when she said to her sister, "Mr. Oates's credit card didn't go through. I tried three times and it was rejected. I'll have to speak with him later."

Angie tossed an angry glance in the man's direction. "He's a real jerk. I hope he doesn't stiff you for the room charges."

Ellie looked surprised. "You think he'd do that? Take off without paying?"

"I wouldn't put anything past him."

Ellie placed some muffins in the box. "I'd better approach him about the payment. I've put it off for a couple of days."

Angie told Ellie what the man said about Bella.

"Maybe he thinks he's funny," Ellie said. "Maybe he has no filter and just says whatever pops into his head."

"What does he do for a living?" Angie asked.

"I have no idea. He never said." Ellie sidled up to her sister. "He's odd, isn't he? He asked me on the first day he arrived not to clean his room, not to bring in fresh towels, not to remove the trash. I told him we needed to remove trash every day from the rooms. He said he'd take his trash down himself. He needed privacy."

Angie crossed her arms over her chest. "Why does he need so much privacy that you can't bring towels into the room or take out the trash on a daily basis?"

Ellie gave a shrug. "Oates told me he has sleep problems. He sleeps at odd times, has to sleep when he's able to. He hoped I'd respect his health issue and not disturb him."

"You think it's legit?"

"Who knows?" Ellie picked up the bakery box. "He's an odd duck, but as long he isn't trashing the room and he's following the inn's rules, he can have his privacy. It's less work for me."

Angie took another quick look at Oates at his table. *An odd duck, indeed.*

16

Jenna worked in her jewelry room at the table in front of the fireplace putting together an intricate gemstone, pearl, and crystal necklace she'd designed for a private order. Sitting back in her chair, she closed her eyes for a few minutes. The close work tired her eyes so on the advice of her optometrist, every thirty minutes, she would look up and across the room for thirty seconds to keep her vision from blurring as she put together the jewelry creations.

As soon as Jenna picked up her tool, Ellie rushed into the room.

"Do you have time to help me out? I have new guests arriving early today and I have three rooms to clean for them on top of the normal housekeeping duties ... and I don't have the afternoon snacks prepared yet either."

Jenna stood up. "Of course, I'll help. The store doesn't open until 10am today so you have me for two hours. What do you want me to do?"

The two sisters left the jewelry shop and headed to the second floor utility closet.

"Could you make up these rooms for me?" Ellie handed a piece of paper to Jenna. "They need the towels changed and the trash taken away. The beds have to made and the ones with asterisks next to them need the sheets changed. And they need to be vacuumed."

Jenna raised an eyebrow. "Maybe I'll rescind my agreement to help."

Ellie looked like she might cry until her sister said, "Just kidding."

"I'll do the other rooms and then I'll go downstairs and prepare the food for the afternoon buffet table." Ellie pulled some linens from the closet and before starting away, she looked back. "Thank you so much. I owe you."

"You sure do," Jenna kidded. "I'll think of some way you can make it up to me."

After tackling the first room, the tall brunette placed the pillows on the bed, glanced around the space at her work, and smiled thinking it looked pretty darned good. *Maybe I'll make Ellie pay me*, she thought with a chuckle.

Pulling her cart to the next room on the list, Jenna pulled out the master key and opened the door carrying in the fresh towels for the bathroom. She emptied the trash and when she started to straighten the sheets and pull up the covers, her foot hit something under the bed.

Jenna knelt on one knee to see what she'd kicked and saw a pair of boots on their sides. Mud was caked on the soles. Not wanting to touch the occupant's things, she stood to finish the bed.

Marvin Oates entered the room and halted at the threshold, his face beet red. "What are you doing in here?" he bellowed.

Startled by the loud voice, Jenna whirled to the man with her mouth hanging open. "I … I'm making up the room."

"You aren't supposed to be in here." Oates crossed to where Jenna stood frozen. "You have no right to come in here."

Anger rose in Jenna's chest. "In fact, as part owner of this establishment, I have every right to enter this room, at any time that I see fit." She took a step towards Oates with her hands on her hips. "If you have an issue with the state code, why don't you call the Attorney General's office and ask for a copy of the rules and regulations pertaining to inns and bed and breakfasts?"

Oates face was practically purple.

Ellie darted into the room. "What's going on?"

"She's in my room." Oates lifted his arm and pointed at Jenna.

"I asked her to clean the room, Mr. Oates. I needed help today and my sister was gracious enough to step in and help me out. In my hurry, I forgot to tell her to leave the towels at your door and not to clean in here. I apologize."

"She shouldn't be in here," Oates was yelling.

Euclid and Circe raced into the room, jumped on the bed, and hissed at the man.

"Good grief." Ellie moved to get the cats.

"Now there are cats in here," Oates boomed. He looked like he might have a stroke. "Get out. Get out of my room."

Euclid swiped at the man with his paw.

Jenna stepped between Oates and the bed and leveled her eyes at the man. "You need to quiet your voice. There are other guests staying here. If you can't control yourself, you need to step into the hallway and collect yourself. My sister explained the situation to you. If that is unacceptable, then you may take your things and leave the inn and I will stand in here while you clear out. It is your choice. If you plan to stay, you will not raise your voice to me or to anyone else in this house. What do you want to do, Mr. Oates?"

Oates's eyes were wild. He coughed and sputtered while his chest rose and fell.

Donald and Lance ran down the stairs from the third floor and hurried into the room.

"You need help in here?" Donald asked. He carried a wrench in his hand.

Lance stood behind his co-worker looking fearful of the yelling, but ready to step in to assist.

Jenna stared at Oates. "*Do* we need help in here?"

Oates swept his eyes from person to person and clenched his fists, but took in a deep breath and tried to calm his tone. "No. Everything is okay."

"Are you staying or have you decided to go elsewhere?" Ellie asked.

"I'm staying, but I'd like you all to leave my room now." Oates ran his hand over his face.

Jenna glared at the man and, as she pushed the vacuum from the room, she called to Euclid and Circe to come with her. Passing Donald and Lance, she whispered thanks.

Ellie gave a grateful nod to the carpenters and turned to speak quietly with Mr. Oates.

On the second floor landing, Jenna was readying the cart for the next room.

"You sure everything is okay?" Donald asked.

Jenna explained what had happened.

"Someone overreacted, it seems," Donald said.

"It seems so. I thought he was going to strike me." Jenna thanked the two men again.

"You need anything, you just yell." Donald led the way back to the third floor.

Jenna bent down and gave the cats a scratch behind their ears. "Thanks for coming to my rescue," she told them with a smile. Looking back at Oates's room, she added, "It takes all kinds, doesn't it?"

Euclid scowled and hissed.

SITTING at her work table again after helping Ellie with the rooms, Jenna yawned as she completed the necklace she'd been working on. The cats snoozed on the sofa by the window and Jenna thought how nice it would be to fall asleep herself. The adrenaline rush she'd experienced in Oates's room had left her feeling fatigued and weak and she considered going to the kitchen for a cup of coffee.

Something in the corner of the room caught her eye and when she saw what it was, she nearly tumbled from her seat.

"Nana," Jenna whispered.

Nana stood still and quiet beside the small Christmas tree, but a warm, loving smile crossed her lips. Her body seemed translucent and glimmered like the sunlight flooding the room.

Circe and Euclid lifted their heads and trilled at the ghost.

"Can you talk to me?" Jenna asked softly.

Nana's head gave the slightest of shakes.

"Can I ask you questions?"

Nana held Jenna's eyes with her own.

"Is Angie in danger?"

The smile fell from Nana's face.

"Can we keep her safe?" Tears welled in the young woman's eyes. "What I saw can be changed, can't it?"

Nana nodded.

A few tears tumbled down Jenna's cheek and she bit her lip and brushed the wetness from her face. "I don't know what to do. I don't know how to keep Angie safe. I don't know who to fear."

Nana turned her eyes to the decorated tree. Reaching for something on one of the branches, she lifted it, looked back at Jenna, and pushed the ornament across the floor to her granddaughter's feet.

Bending, Jenna picked up the object and looked at it. "I don't understand."

Nana put her hand on her heart and then her form became softer and full of light, until she disappeared.

"Don't go," Jenna whispered as the tears fell from her eyes. "Don't leave me. I don't know what to do."

17

Jenna sat at the kitchen table with Angie and Mr. Finch telling them about the visit from Nana's spirit.

"Then she picked something off the Christmas tree and pushed it across the floor to me. This is the thing she rolled." Jenna placed an ornament in the center of the table. It was a little boot with a candy cane, sprigs of greenery, and a white cat peeking out the top of it.

"What does it mean?" Angie asked.

"It has to be a clue of some kind," Finch said. "Otherwise, why would your nana choose to bring this to your attention?"

Jenna said, "I asked Nana if my visions show future situations that are set in stone or are they only what *might* be? She nodded when I asked if we can impact future events. I told her I didn't know what to do to keep Angie safe. That's when she chose the ornament from the tree and pushed it over the floor to me."

"I, too, believe our actions make the future what it will be," Finch said. "We have to figure out what the little boot ornament means."

Angie picked up the ornament and turned it in her hand. "Do we need to be careful of someone wearing a boot?"

Jenna sighed. "It's cold and snowy here. Almost everyone in town is wearing boots."

"It doesn't exactly narrow down the list of suspects," Angie frowned.

"Is the clue something more subtle?" Finch asked. "Is it the white cat?"

"We don't know any white cats," Jenna said.

Finch raised an eyebrow. "Maybe there's one in our future."

Angie got up and brought over a cranberry-apple pie she'd made that morning. "Let's eat the pie and have some tea. Thinking requires energy."

Jenna put her fork down and sipped her tea. "I have to tell you about something that happened this morning."

Finch and Angie stared wide-eyed as Jenna

relayed her run-in with Marvin Oates. "He was acting crazy, obsessive. I didn't know he'd arranged with Ellie not to have his room cleaned and she forgot to mention it to me. It was like I'd stolen from him or something. He was outraged that I'd entered his personal space."

"The man is rude and just plain odd," Angie said. "He had no right to overreact like that."

Sighing, Jenna said, "I could have handled it better, but I was so angry and annoyed by his behavior. This is our house. He is a guest here. There was no need to fly off the handle like that." Picking up her tea cup, she added, "It made me feel really bad. Like I had done something terrible. Like I lost control of my temper."

"We've all been under strain the past week," Angie told her sister. "Oates was out of line to confront you like that. You didn't do anything wrong."

"It was very good of Donald and Lance to come downstairs from the renovation work to see if you needed any help," Finch said.

"Oh, yes. I told them how much I appreciated it." Jenna lifted another forkful of pie. "Oates made such a fuss, they could hear him up on the third floor."

A knock on the backdoor sounded and Angie

went to answer it finding Chief Martin on the rear steps holding a leather folder.

"I have a little bit of news, nothing Earth shattering, but I thought I'd tell you about it." The chief sat at the table and Angie brought him coffee and a slice of pie. With a smile, the man said, "It seems the Roselands are always feeding me lately."

"We're glad to. We have to keep up your strength." Jenna chuckled.

"Analysis was done on some of the boot prints left by the Peeping Tom at different scenes. Unfortunately, nothing viable was recovered from the spot where Bella Masters was attacked." The chief removed some photographs from his folder. "These are some photos of the tread from the boots. It's a distinctive pattern and points to a particular brand. Of course, it is a very popular brand of boots which doesn't exactly narrow things down." The man pointed to part of the tread marks in the photographs. "But, see here? This part of the boots' soles is worn in an irregular pattern which tells us the perpetrator's feet are prone to the outside."

"So if you could find the pair of boots of this brand and with this pattern of wear, it would narrow down the suspects," Jenna observed.

"It would, yes." Chief Martin gave a nod. "It's not a heck of a lot, but it's something."

Jenna suddenly sat at attention. "Oh."

"What is it?" the chief asked.

Pointing to the ornament on the table, she looked at the chief. "This ornament. It...." She stopped and thought how to better explain about the boot ornament.

Angie said, "Our nana paid Jenna a visit a couple of hours ago."

The chief's posture stiffened. It didn't matter that the man knew about the Roselands' skills and about ghosts and *feelings* and premonitions, it always caught him off guard. "Did she?"

"Nana took this ornament from the tree in my shop and pushed it across the floor to me. It was a clue, but we didn't know what it meant. Now, we do."

"She was trying to tell us to look for a particular pair of boots," Angie added.

"Of course, it is like searching for a needle in a haystack," Finch said, "but it is an important piece of information that will lead us in the right direction ... and eventually to the criminal."

Angie gave Finch a warm smile for being so hopeful and positive and then looked to the chief.

"Have there been any new incidents with the Peeping Tom showing up anywhere?"

"None." Chief Martin finished his slice of pie. "But that doesn't give us any hope he's moved on or has given up. We see it as him relishing and reveling in his attack on Ms. Masters. When his "high" from the attack fades, we believe he will up his activity."

Angie's heart sank at this news. "Then we have to figure this out ... and soon."

Jenna asked, "Does the sole's tread seen in these photos indicate the boot is either a man's or a woman's?"

"Not really. The shoe could be either. The size is a little bigger than the average women's boot and slightly smaller than the average man's size boot. Even if it was a man's boot, nothing prevents a woman from wearing them, as we saw from the last case we worked on together." Chief Martin was referring to a recent murder case where the killer, a woman, wore men's athletic shoes in a larger size than what she regularly wore in order to throw off the police's consideration of possible suspects.

"So we can't rule out a woman being the Peeping Tom," Mr. Finch said.

"That's right."

A woman's voice called from the hallway. "Ellie?"

Elizabeth Winters appeared in the doorway of the kitchen. "Sorry to bother. I'm looking for Ellie."

"Ellie's gone out to the market, but will be back shortly," Angie told the woman. "Is there anything we can help you with?"

"I've run out of shampoo and wondered if she could give me another bottle," Elizabeth said.

Mr. Finch made quick eye contact with Angie and stood. "I'd be happy to get some for you." Finch picked up his cane and headed for the supply closet off the kitchen. "Is there anything else you need?"

"Maybe another towel."

"Right-o," Finch said. He took the two items from the closet and walked over to where Elizabeth was standing at the doorway. "Any of us are happy to help you, if you cannot find Miss Ellie." Finch gave the woman a warm smile. "I don't believe we have been formally introduced. I am Victor Finch, a friend of the family." He extended his hand to shake with the woman.

"Elizabeth Winters." The woman shook with the older man and then took the shampoo and towel and headed for her room. "Thanks for your help."

"Anytime." Finch gave the woman a nod and then returned to join the others at the kitchen table.

"Clever of you, Mr. Finch." Angie winked.

"Always thinking." Finch tapped his forehead with his index finger.

Leaning forward, Jenna asked, "Did you pick up on anything?"

"I did." Finch hung the crook of his cane over the edge of the table. "Ms. Winters is in a state of mental distress."

The chief's eyebrows shot up, amazed at what Finch was able to sense in only a few seconds.

"Really?" Angie asked with a tone of surprise. "Why? What's causing it?"

"Her work, perhaps. Her mind is a jumble. Tension and stress run through her like a rushing river. I felt anxiety, unease, worry, anger, resentment."

"Wow," Jenna said. "The woman is a mess."

"When she arrived at the B and B," Angie said, "she told me she is always stressed out at this time of year and she takes two or three weeks off to try and decompress."

"According to Mr. Finch, her vacation doesn't seem to be helping her," Jenna pointed out.

"Maybe her work situation is causing her major stress," Finch offered.

"What does Ms. Winters do?" the chief asked.

"She told me she was a vice president at a financial firm," Angie said.

"Well, that must be a source of plenty of stress," Chief Martin said.

Jenna narrowed her eyes. "Could her anxiety and anger be an indication of something more?"

"Meaning criminal behavior?" Angie asked.

"Could she be the Peeping Tom?" Jenna suggested. "She arrived in the area around the time the Peeping Tom started his activities."

The muscles around the chief's mouth tensed. "At this point, no one can be ruled out." He made eye contact with Angie. "Don't be alone around the woman."

Angie let out a nervous sigh.

18

It was almost 5pm when Angie, working late in the shop to prepare some baked goods for the next morning, heard a thud when a strong wind blew the wreath off the bake shop's door. She stepped out onto the porch and picked up the evergreen wreath to see that the hook had ripped off the back. Leaning it on the porch railing, Angie noticed Lance sitting in the bed of his truck pulling on his athletic shoes.

She gave him a wave. "My wreath broke. The wind knocked it off the door."

He gave her a shy look. "Want me to see if I can fix it?"

Surprised by the offer, Angie hesitated for a moment and then said, "Sure, thanks." She carried it over to the truck. "See, the hook part that attached to the door broke off."

Lance took the wreath, placed it in the bed of his truck, and opened a small tool box. He took some wire and a pliers and bent over the wreath forming a new hook on the back of the decoration. "I think that will work." He handed it back to Angie.

"That was quick. Thanks a bunch." She smiled at the young man, but he looked away from her pretending to fiddle with his tools.

Lance hurried to the driver's side of his truck, opened the door, and took out a jacket and slipped it on. It was clear to Angie that their exchange was now over, but before she started towards the bake shop door, she noticed Lance's boots in the truck bed. She squinted at them.

The tread on the soles looked to match the pattern on the ones in the photographs Chief Martin showed them. The soles seemed to be worn down more at the edges, just like the ones in the photos.

A flash of nerves ran through Angie's body. She hurried to the porch, her hands clammy with cold sweat.

BUNDLED IN WINTER JACKETS, hats and gloves, Jenna, Angie, Courtney, and Ellie walked up Beach Street to the main street of town. Snow flurries floated in the air and sparkled under the old-fashioned street-lamps. More people than usual wandered the streets looking in store windows, carrying shopping bags, and heading out to restaurants and pubs.

"I love the Holiday Stroll." Courtney pulled her hat down around her ears. "I love seeing people's decorations."

"Me, too." Ellie chuckled. "I think we enjoy it so much because we're all nosey about other people's houses."

The Holiday Stroll was a fundraiser for the Sweet Cove historical preservation society where each year ten home owners opened their houses to townspeople and tourists to come inside to see how they'd decorated for the holiday season. Most home owners put out cookies and drinks for the strollers to enjoy.

The preservation society considered cancelling the tour this year due to the trouble going on in town, but people wanted it to go forward saying if the tour was canceled, then the town would be giving into a criminal and then the criminal would win. Townspeople hoped the stroll would bring some much needed cheer to everyone.

Angie said, "With everything going on, I forgot to tell you that I was approached by someone at the preservation society to put the Victorian on the list of homes on the holiday stroll for next year."

Courtney let out a whoop. "That's great." She looked at Angie with concern. "You did say *yes*, didn't you?"

Angie smiled. "I did."

"We'll have to do the decorations up big next year," Courtney said. "We'll need to start planning early. We all need to look closely at the houses this year to see what they've done." Rubbing her hands together, the youngest sister said, "I can't wait. This is going to be fun."

Jenna said, "We have the Holiday Charity Gala at the resort in a few days. I'm looking forward to it."

"It's the only time we get to wear gowns," Courtney smiled, "and the guys have to wear tuxes. Except when there's a wedding."

Ellie eyed Angie. "Maybe a couple we know will set a date soon?"

Angie said with a half-smile, "Maybe."

The family had a long discussion about whether Angie should attend crowded events and after much going back and forth, it was agreed it would be safe for her to go to things since she would be with family members and friends. The final decision was Angie's and she thought everything would be fine with people around her.

THE SISTERS APPROACHED the first house on the tour, a two-and-a-half story brick Georgian with a stone walkway that led to the front door. Two tall trees decorated with ribbons, bows, and ornaments stood on each side of the entryway like handsome sentries welcoming people to the house. An enormous wreath covered with colorful glass balls and ribbon hung on the door. The Juliet porch on the second floor of the home had graceful garlands of evergreens decorating the wrought-iron railing.

Ellie stared at the grand home. "Gorgeous."

"Well, if this is what the outside looks like," Jenna said, "I can't wait to see the inside."

The sisters entered and had their tickets stamped before proceeding through the foyer, the living room, dining room, sunroom, family room, and kitchen. Each room was elaborately decorated with trees, garland, table settings, angels, ribbon, and flowers. On the landing from the first floor to the second floor, a brass band was set up and playing holiday tunes.

On the massive kitchen island, platters of cookies, squares, and slices of breads covered the surface. Hot cocoa, teas, and coffee, along with hot cider were set up on another long counter. The kitchen was decorated with a sparkling tall, slender tree in the corner and ropes of garland hung over the tops of the cabinetry.

"Wow," Courtney whispered to Angie, "we'll have our work cut out for us next year. This place is fabulous."

A shudder of worry gripped Angie's stomach as she hoped she would stay safe and be able to look forward to having a next year. A terrible sense of unease washed over her and dampened her mood.

"Want some hot cocoa, Angie?" Ellie asked.

Before Angie could reply, a piercing scream that came from the family room shook the house, sending a ripple of panic through the crowd visiting the home.

The Roseland sisters ran in the direction of the scream and found two women being comforted by a few of the tour-goers.

"What happened?" Jenna demanded.

"There was a man." A short, stout woman with

silver gray hair pointed at the big window that over-looked the backyard. Terror showed on her face and her shoulders shook. She put her hand over her mouth.

Part of the yard was lit by a security light, but the section just outside the window was cloaked in shadows.

Angie asked the other woman who was gray-haired, taller, and slim, "You saw a man in the yard?"

"Yes." The woman had her hand over her heart.

"What did you see?"

The woman's voice was hoarse. "He had a knife."

"What did he do?" Angie used a steady voice to try and help calm the woman.

"He held it up in a menacing way."

"Could you see his face?"

"He had on a black ski jacket. The hood was pulled up and the ties were pulled tight so the fabric covered his face."

"Please call the police," Angie asked the couple standing next to the woman and then she and her sisters returned to the kitchen to find the rear door. "Don't let anyone go out back. The police will need to see the footprints the man left behind."

A volunteer from the preservation society placed

herself in front of the door to block anyone from exiting that way.

It was only about fifteen minutes before Chief Martin and two other officers arrived at the house. One officer went to interview the women who saw the man with the knife. Chief Martin, the other officer carrying a camera, and the Roseland sisters left the house to inspect the rear garden.

"Let's all be careful of the footprints," the chief warned. "Here they are right near the window to the room where the women were standing." Chief Martin bent at the waist to get a closer look at the prints in the snow. "The snow is crisp and icy back here, not great for getting a good print." He instructed the officer to take some photos.

The chief's eyes ran along the yard to the property line at the side where some of the footprints could be seen heading into the woods. "There are some partial footprints going into the tree line. From the distance between the prints, it looks like the guy was running."

"The creep is playing with people, trying to frighten them by appearing at the holiday stroll, showing them the knife," Jenna grumped. "He must be a real sicko."

"He is certainly bold showing up at this event."

Ellie's voice was hoarse with anger as she looked over the footprints in the snow.

"Do the prints match the ones you've found in other yards where the Peeping Tom has shown up?" Courtney asked the chief.

"There are similarities in the tread on the soles, but the lighting is poor and lots of people wear similar kinds of boots. We'll have the tech people take a look and see what they think."

When the other officer stepped to the tree line to photograph the prints there, the chief asked quietly, "Any of you pick up on anything?"

"I felt anxious right before the woman screamed," Angie admitted. "But that doesn't provide us any clues."

"I don't feel anything," Courtney said with disappointment.

"Neither do I." Jenna kicked at the snow.

"Ellie? Anything?" the chief asked.

The security light shined on the back of Ellie's long blond hair making it look almost white. She had her hands in her pockets and her eyes glued to the spot where the perpetrator had run into the woods.

"Ellie?" Angie asked her sister.

Ellie blinked and shook herself.

"Are you able to pick up on anything?" the chief repeated his question.

Ellie turned her blue eyes to Chief Martin and took a few moments before answering. "I think we know this person."

Everyone's jaws dropped.

19

Ellie didn't actually mean that they knew the Peeping Tom well, but she was sure they'd met him ... or her. "I'm sure of it. I could feel it. We've met this person."

"Well, that narrows it down," Courtney said. "How many people have we all met? Thousands? Tens of thousands?"

Ellie ignored the comment. "I feel like we've met the person fairly recently."

The group was back at the mansion sitting together in the kitchen. Angie had started to bake something since whenever she needed to think over a problem, the act of baking helped her mind settle.

"What are you making?" Courtney moved from the table to the kitchen island.

"A chocolate-peppermint cheesecake." Angie measured out the flour.

Courtney let out a contented sigh. "I can go on living."

Angie said, "I told Chief Martin about Lance's boots. The soles looked worn on one edge and the pattern in the treads seemed similar to what we saw in the crime photographs." She stopped what she was doing and looked across the room. "I don't know. I just don't get the feeling Lance is involved in this stuff."

"Why not?" Jenna questioned.

Angie shrugged. "I'm not sure. He seems sort of normal, I mean, even though his shyness seems paralyzing. I would cross him off the list of suspects."

"Nope," Courtney said. "He stays on until we know something for sure. We're not going to let our guard down with anyone."

"Fine." Angie returned to the work of chopping the fine chocolate.

"Is the Peeping Tom asking to be found out?" Ellie poured tea for everyone. "He seems to be taking stupid chances. Showing up at a house filled with volunteers and tour guests? It doesn't seem like a smart thing to do. Too many people, too many chances for someone to identify him."

Finch pondered. "Perhaps, the thrill of frightening so many people was desperately hard for him to resist."

"He's really a sicko." Courtney sipped from her mug. "I'd love to get my hands on him."

Euclid and Circe sat on top of the refrigerator listening to the conversation.

"The guy is becoming more and more bold," Jenna said. "He's escalated from peeping in people's windows to killing someone, and he taunted all of us at the house stroll."

"It's worrisome." Feeling vulnerable, Ellie made eye contact with Jenna and then took a quick glance at Angie. If the Peeping Tom was becoming less careful, was taking more chances, was becoming so bold and arrogant, was the danger to Angie increasing? "It has me feeling nervous."

"No worries, sis," Courtney said. "We're all together. We can handle this guy."

"But we're not all together all the time," Ellie said. "We can't keep an eye on each other every minute of every day."

Angie looked up from the baking. "I'll be okay. I'm being careful. I watch everyone like a hawk. I'm always ready to run or fight." The young woman sighed. "I always loved this time of year ... until now."

Ellie went to her sister and wrapped her in her arms. "Things will get better," she said softly, hoping her words were true.

"Where's Mr. Finch?" Jenna asked.

"He's at home," Courtney said. "I texted him to let him know what happened at the holiday stroll. He's coming over in a little bit."

"When he comes, we need to put our heads together," Jenna said. "This mess has been going on too long."

The backdoor opened as if on cue and Finch entered the kitchen after removing his hat and coat. "It's bitter cold out there." Finch leaned on his cane and crossed to the table where he took a seat. He carried his sketchbook under his arm.

"Let's get you some tea." Jenna poured the liquid into a mug and brought it to the older man.

"We're discussing what happened," Ellie told him. She gave a rundown of the event with her sisters chiming in with details. Ellie explained that she got the sense they'd met the Peeping Tom. "And then we came home after talking with Chief Martin."

Finch's caterpillar brows pinched together. "The perpetrator is getting quite bold."

"My very words," Ellie nodded in agreement. "Let's consider suspects."

Angie shifted her gaze to her sister. "You're not shying away from this case like you usually do."

Ellie straightened, pushed her shoulders back, and made eye contact with Angie. "No, I'm not. My sister might be in danger."

Angie smiled at the sister who preferred to have nothing to do with paranormal things, crimes, or criminals, unless one of her own was in trouble.

Finch asked the young blonde, "Do you feel that we have all met the criminal or are you the only one who has made his acquaintance?"

Ellie thought about the question, thinking things over. "I think we've all met the person."

"Do you have any sense if the criminal is a man or a woman?" Jenna questioned.

Ellie's face clouded. "I'm not sure. I don't lean one way or the other."

"Mr. Finch has picked up a few things by shaking hands with Elizabeth Winters," Courtney said. "He sensed tension and stress, anger and resentment from her. But is the anger and stress enough to push her into committing crimes?"

"That would take more sleuthing," Finch admitted.

"What about Lance and his boots?" Courtney asked. "Angie thinks he's innocent, but I'm not so quick to eliminate him. We still don't know why he had a newspaper clipping about Angie in his tool-box. That's weird, isn't it? Why are we ignoring that?"

"We aren't ignoring it," Angie said as she switched off the food processor. "Lance does his work. He doesn't bother anyone. There's probably a good explanation for why he has that clipping."

Jenna said, "Why don't we ask Tom to talk to Lance about it? Ask him why he has that news clipping? Then we'll have the answer and we don't have to speculate anymore."

"Okay," Angie agreed with reluctance.

"I also shook hands with Lance," Finch reminded the group. "He had on gloves and the handshake was brief. I felt sadness, loss, a fear of the world, and not knowing who to trust. I did not feel anger or hostility or revenge, all things I would expect to feel from a killer."

"What about Elizabeth Winters?" Courtney said. "You felt anger from her."

"The sensations were mixed together," Finch

said. "She seemed resentful, confused, adrift. I don't think what I sensed indicated a killer."

"What about that crazy Marvin Oates?" Jenna made a face. "He seems obsessive. I had the run-in with him over cleaning his room. His response was over the top. He seems wacky." Jenna turned to Mr. Finch. "Have you shaken Oates's hand?"

"I have not, but it seems I should," Finch said.

"You think Oates has something in his room that he doesn't want anyone to see?" Courtney's eyes had a look of excitement. "Maybe we should try to clean his room in the morning, when he's having breakfast or when he goes out."

"No way." Jenna shook her head. "Absolutely not. I'm not going in that man's room ever again."

Courtney eyed Ellie.

An expression of horror washed over Ellie's face and she held her hand up with the palm side out. "Oh, no. Not me. I can't go into his room."

"What about me?" Angie asked.

"Absolutely not," Courtney said. "We aren't putting the one person who is supposed to be in danger in harm's way. You get to sit this one out, sis."

"What about me?" Finch looked impish. "I could play the doddering old man. I could get confused about what room I'm in and wander into Oates's room instead … and then have a look around."

"The only problem with that is," Ellie said, "Oates doesn't leave his door unlocked. Jenna had the master key to go in to clean. If Oates caught you in his room, there'd be no way to explain how you got in there."

"I could say he forgot to lock his door," Finch suggested.

"He would never fall for that," Ellie said. "He is meticulous in locking the door."

"We'll just have to sneak in," Finch winked. "Think about it."

When Angie finished the cheesecake and slipped it into the oven, Finch cleared his throat. "I made some drawings this evening."

Jenna looked pained.

"I thought it might be a good idea if Miss Jenna had a look." Finch reached for the sketchbook and slid it across the table to the brunette. "Whenever you feel up to it. It doesn't have to be now."

"It's okay. I'll do it. Let's see if the pictures give us any new information." As Jenna took in some deep breaths, Angie ambled over to the island and sat on the stool next to Courtney, then swiveled it so she could watch her twin.

Jenna began slowly turning the pages. She paused at one of them, a drawing of the Victorian's living room. Immediately, the ring of fire formed in the center and within the ring, Jenna saw a little girl playing with a dollhouse. The dollhouse was an exact replica of the Victorian.

For several moments, the little girl, Gigi, stared back at Jenna, and then she reached her hand out and opened the tiny front door of the house.

Jenna gasped.

Angie lay on the foyer floor, unconscious, her hand covering her stomach. Blood pooled on the floor beside her.

Gigi looked back at Jenna with tears streaming down her cheeks.

Jenna leaned forward. The staircase leading down to the foyer was visible. Someone stood near the top of stairs. Jenna could only see the person's legs.

The person was wearing work boots.

The ring of fire faded and Jenna swayed in her seat until Ellie reached over to put her arm around her sister's shoulders to steady her.

Jenna's head lolled around, her eyes rolled back in her head, and she passed out.

20

After Jenna revived and told the family what she'd seen in the drawing, Tom came to the Victorian to bring her home. He called in the morning to tell them that Jenna was exhausted and was sleeping in, but would come later in the day to open her jewelry shop.

Angie had a couple of hours before heading to work in the bake shop and was helping Ellie prepare the B and B guests' breakfast buffet.

"This whole thing is taking a toll on Jenna," Ellie said as she placed hard-boiled eggs into a red and green bowl. "And I worry about Mr. Finch. Betty told me he becomes so engrossed in the drawings that he forgets to eat. She doesn't know that any of us have powers, she thinks he's just obsessed with making art. I think Mr. Finch feels the need to do as much as he can to solve this thing and keep you safe so he pushes himself to fatigue."

Angie put a variety of muffins into a basket. "It makes me feel very guilty. Everyone is working so hard to help me."

Ellie reached over and gently touched her sister's shoulder. "I didn't bring this up to make you feel guilty. We'd all work day and night to help one of us. If it was me who was in danger, I know you'd do anything for me. Am I right?"

Angie gave a little nod.

"It's your turn to accept our care and love ... without feeling guilty." Ellie looked tenderly at her sister. "And you'll be there to help when one of us needs it." A grin formed over Ellie's face. "But since you're feeling guilty, I have a way for you to make it up to me. Help me clean the guest rooms this morning."

Angie chuckled. "Hmm, let me think about that. Maybe, I'm not feeling guilty at all now."

Ellie bopped Angie's arm and went back to making the breakfasts.

Once the food was put in the dining room, and several guests came down to eat, Ellie talked Angie into helping her with the rooms. The two sisters and the cats headed up the staircase to the second floor.

"Whatever you do, don't go into Marvin Oates's room. We don't need a repeat of the other day," Ellie warned as she pulled the housekeeping push cart and the vacuum cleaners out of the storage closet. "I'll handle him."

Euclid flattened his ears and hissed.

"I'll steer clear, don't worry." Angie removed fresh towels and linens from the linen closet.

"The guests in rooms 3, 6, and 8 are already downstairs eating breakfast so let's tackle those rooms first." Ellie pulled the master key from her pocket. "We'll work together instead of splitting up. I don't want you alone up here."

They entered the first room where they dusted and vacuumed, cleaned the bathroom, took out the trash, made the bed, and replaced the linens. Ellie checked the flowers to see if they had to be changed. She always put fresh flowers in each room along with a variety of teas, coffee, water bottles, chocolates, and cookies.

The cats sat at the threshold looking in. They weren't allowed in the rooms as Ellie didn't think any of the guests would appreciate cat hair on the floor or the beds.

"Okay, one down." Ellie announced as she shut

and locked the door and moved the cart down the hallway to the next room.

"Too many more to go," Angie teased.

After opening the next room's door so Angie could get started, Ellie carried new towels to put on the small side table outside of Marvin Oates's room. Every morning, Oates put the trash out when he left and Ellie put towels and toiletries on the table for him to take into his room. She hoped he wasn't doing anything illegal in there and wished she could take a peek to be sure everything looked okay.

"When is Oates scheduled to checkout?" Angie asked when Ellie came into the guest room she was cleaning.

"He was going to leave the B and B tomorrow, but he's extended his time here for another week."

Angie made a sour face. "You had space for him? Aren't all the rooms booked?"

"Unfortunately, I had a cancellation and his room was available." Ellie dusted the desk and side tables. "So I gave it to him."

"I'll be glad when some of these people leave," Angie groaned. "I also will be happy to see the renovations complete and the workers out of the house."

Ellie sighed. "But you don't think Lance is a suspect, do you?"

"I don't. I can't explain it. I don't think he has ill intentions." Angie stripped the bed and prepared to put new sheets on it.

"What about Elizabeth Winters?" Ellie kept her voice quiet.

"I don't know what to think about her. Mr. Finch felt anger and anxiety from her. She's one to watch I guess." Angie paused while tucking in the sheets. "It still bothers me that we found the master key to the guest rooms outside under the tree that night when Courtney and I saw someone standing out there in the dark."

"Like I said, I think it fell out of my pocket one evening when I was preparing the fire pit for the guests. I have three keys hanging on the wall in my office. I didn't even notice one was missing."

"What if one of the guests took it?" Angie asked.

"For what reason?" Ellie put new chocolates on the table.

"To steal from the other guests? Use the key to get into their rooms and steal things?"

"No one has complained that any of their things are missing."

"Maybe whoever stole the key dropped it outside before he could use it," Angie said.

"I think it was in my pocket and fell out when I

was out in the yard." Ellie shrugged. "It's the simplest and most likely explanation. That key is only the master for the rooms here in the main house. It doesn't open the two apartments in the carriage house. If it did, I'd be more concerned about it, afraid someone was trying to get to you."

Angie guessed Ellie was probably right about the key.

"Let's do Elizabeth Winters's room next," Ellie suggested. "She has the *Housekeeping, Please* tag on her doorknob.

The young women and the cats moved to Ms. Winters's room and started the same process of cleaning the space.

"You need to hire a new part-time housekeeper to help out," Angie said. "It's too much for you to handle everything on your own."

"I know. I really liked that last woman who worked here. I'm sorry she moved away. I haven't had time with the holiday rush to even think about hiring someone new. I'll start interviewing in January."

Euclid had been sitting at the room's threshold next to Circe watching Angie and Ellie clean, when he suddenly darted into the room and ran under the bed.

The orange flash caught Angie's eye. "Euclid, you know you can't be in here."

Ellie bent down to look under the bed. "What are you doing, Euclid?"

The cat hissed.

"Has he lost his mind?" Ellie asked her sister. "Come on out. You can't be under there."

While Euclid was under the bed, Circe entered the room and padded quickly to the closet, undetected. The closet hadn't fully shut and she used both her front paws to push at the door so it would open all the way.

Euclid darted from under the bed to Circe's side.

"You two are full of mischief this morning." When Angie walked over to them, the small black cat stepped into the closet and poked at a blanket crumpled on the floor.

Angie moved the blanket and her eyes widened.

On the floor of Elizabeth Winter's closet, were two boots, one on its side. They were the same brand that the perpetrator wore. The sole looked slightly worn on the edges. Mud clung to the bottoms and sides of the boots.

"Ellie," Angie said softly.

The tone of Angie's voice sent a chill along Ellie's spine. "What's wrong?"

Angie pointed and when Ellie looked, she let out a gasp. "Boots? The same brand as the criminal wears?" Her hand covered her mouth as stared at the footwear.

"Have you ever seen Ms. Winters wearing these boots?" Angie asked.

"No. I look at people's feet now to see if they're wearing boots like these. Ms. Winters wears black boots up to the knee. They have fur inside and a zipper. I've never seen these boots before."

The two sisters stared at each other.

"Ms. Winters?" Ellie asked. "Is she...?"

Footsteps could be heard in the hallway. Angie hurriedly kicked at the blanket so it would cover the boots and she closed the closet door just as Elizabeth Winters appeared in the doorway.

"Oh, you're still cleaning," the woman said. "I went out to do some shopping in town, but I have a headache coming on. I'm going to rest."

"We're all done in here," Ellie said forcing a smile. "We'll be out of your way in a second." She scurried into the bathroom to gather the cleaning supplies while Angie pushed the vacuum into the hall.

"Sorry you're not feeling well," Angie said.

"A nap will help." Elizabeth removed her wool coat and tossed it on the chair.

"All set." Ellie hurried out of the room to join Angie and the cats in the hall. "Hope you feel better." She pulled the door shut behind her and let out a long breath. "That was close."

They moved down to the end of the hallway.

Ellie's cheeks had lost their rosy color. "Is she? Is she the killer?"

With a shudder, Angie glanced back to Ms. Winters's room. "We need to talk to Chief Martin."

21

W hen the Roselands, Mr. Finch and Betty, Jack, Tom, and Rufus arrived at the holiday gala at the resort, Josh hurried to them and wrapped Angie in his arms. The men wore tuxedos and the women wore long gowns and their eyes lit up when they entered the grand ballroom to see the space decorated like a winter wonderland.

Ice sculptures, gigantic flower arrangements, Christmas trees, evergreen garland, strings of twinkling lights, and bows and ribbons decorated the room under the huge crystal chandeliers. Waitstaff paraded around the space with trays of champagne and platters of hors d'oeuvres presenting the food and drinks to the party-goers.

"It's beautiful," Angie told her fiancé.

"We'll raise a lot of money for charity." Josh took Angie's hand and led the group to their table. "We have the largest turnout ever this year."

An orchestra played on the stage to the side and people moved across the dance floor to the music. A projector shone against one wall making it look like snowflakes were falling in the room.

"I chose this table for all of us. It's in the corner, but close to two exits, just in case." He squeezed Angie's hand and whispered, "There are plain-clothes security guards in place to keep an eye on you."

Angie didn't think the danger would come as an attack on her. It had seemed to her since the beginning that it would take the form of an attack on someone else and she would get hurt either because she got in the way or because she tried to help the criminal's target.

Despite the precautions Josh had taken, Angie was on edge and uncomfortable, but she put on a happy face and downplayed her feelings so that the evening would go well and the family would enjoy themselves.

Courtney and Rufus took to the dance floor and Ellie and Jack went to talk to some friends. Jenna and Tom wandered around the ballroom looking at the decorations.

Josh had to tend to some questions posed by the chef and promised to return shortly.

Mr. Finch stood close by Angie's side while Betty made the rounds of the room to chat with current and possible clients and other business people.

"Have you all divided the evening up into time slots where each of you have been assigned to stay with me for a certain amount of time?" Angie asked Finch with a sideways glance.

"Now why would you think that?" Finch asked with a sly grin.

"I thought so." Angie smiled at the older man. "What about the cats? Are they lurking somewhere in here?"

Finch returned the smile. "We tried to find a proper place for Euclid and Circe to keep an eye out in the ballroom, but nothing worked well enough so the cats are at home."

Angie chuckled. "They must not be happy about being left out."

"Would you like to stroll around, Miss Angie? Josh told me there are fifty Christmas trees in the room off the ballroom and in the back hallway. Shall we go see?"

"I'd love to." Angie slipped her arm through Finch's and they walked slowly to see the trees.

The low-lit room looked like a forest at night. A pathway looped around the trees in such a way that people seemed to be alone on the paths. Stars and a moon were projected on the ceiling and falling snowflakes showed on all the walls. Artificial snow covered the floor under the trees and soft instrumental music played over the speakers.

"It's so peaceful," Angie said.

"They've done a magnificent job." Finch glanced around in wonder as the two followed the walkway to admire the snowy woodland.

When they completed the stroll and were returning to the ballroom, Angie spotted a man and a woman across the space standing close to one another engaged in an argument. From the expressions on their faces, it was clear that they were furious with one another. The woman gestured angrily and the man leaned forward in a menacing way.

"It's Elizabeth Winters and Marvin Oates." Angie indicated where Finch should look.

"And they are not happy with one another," Finch observed.

A group of people crossed Angie's and Finch's

line of vision and when they passed by, Winters and Oates were gone.

"What was that all about?" Finch asked.

"Good question." The argument had sent flashes of panic through Angie's body. "Could those two be working together? Could they both be the Peeping Tom?"

Finch's mouth opened, but he didn't speak. He took Angie's elbow and propelled her down the hall and back into the ballroom to their table.

Jenna and Tom saw them approaching and relief washed over their faces.

"We wondered where you had gone." Jenna let out a tense breath.

"We were just about to send out a search party," Tom said.

Angie explained what they'd seen in the hall and expressed her suspicion that Winters and Oates might possibly be working together.

"I never considered that." Jenna looked around the ballroom to see if she could see them. "Are they in here? Does anyone see them?"

"Maybe they left," Finch offered. "But here comes someone else."

Wearing a tuxedo, Chief Martin strode across the room towards them. "Evening."

Angie and Finch reported seeing Winters and Oates arguing in another room.

"Interesting." The chief rubbed his chin. "I have some news as well. After Angie and Ellie told me about the boots in Elizabeth Winters's room, we did some research on the woman."

"Please don't tell us everything she said to us is a lie," Jenna moaned.

"It isn't, but she left out some important details. Ms. Winters is indeed a vice president of a financial firm in Boston. She has recently suffered losses. Her mother passed away not long ago from a serious illness. Ms. Winters's husband died a month ago in a private plane crash."

"How terrible," Angie said.

"I spoke with Ms. Winters's colleague and superior. He said Elizabeth is distraught by the losses. He had high praise for her as a person and as a professional. Elizabeth is having a very difficult time coping with the situation and this man, a president at the firm, insisted she take a month off from work to rest and seek grief counseling. She was pushing herself to mental exhaustion and he feared for her own health."

"So she came to the North Shore to give herself a

break from the misery and give herself a chance to rest," Jenna said. "The poor woman."

"So she is not a suspect then," Finch said.

The chief didn't speak, only made eye contact with the people around him.

"What?" Angie asked. "She *is* a suspect?"

The chief said, "Mental anguish can trigger issues. It can cause people to do things out of character. Ms. Winters could be spiraling out of control."

"She *could* be the Peeping Tom? She *could* be the killer?" Tom asked.

"We can't dismiss the possibility yet," Chief Martin said. "I need to speak with Ms. Winters. Is she still here? Have you seen her again?"

"We haven't," Finch said.

"Isn't that her over there?" Jenna gestured. "It is. There she goes."

"I'll go see if I can talk to her." The chief headed off across the crowded room.

Angie sank onto a chair and put her forehead in her hand.

"Are you okay?" Jenna sat next to her sister.

"I'm tired. My head hurts. I think I'd like to go home. Can I take your car? You can all pile into Ellie's van when you leave."

"I'll go home with you," Jenna said.

"Please don't. Stay. I'll go back and rest. I feel like I'm coming down with a bad cold."

"I don't want you to be alone."

"I won't be alone. The B and B guests are there." Angie gave a weak smile. "The cats are there, too. It will make me feel badly if you miss the rest of the gala. Please stay. I'll be fine. I won't go to the carriage house apartment until Courtney returns. I'll stay in the Victorian. I'll go to Ellie's room and rest on her bed."

Jenna reluctantly agreed and took her car key from her purse and handed it to Angie. "We won't stay long."

"Stay until the end. I'll be asleep anyway. Tell Courtney to wake me up when she gets back. Tell Josh I'm sorry I had to leave." Angie took the key and gave her sister, Tom, and Finch a hug. "Don't fret over me. Stay and have fun."

Tom walked Angie to the car.

Jenna said to Finch, "I keep seeing flashes of the vision I had where Gigi was playing with dollhouse. I can see the boots on the staircase in the foyer. Each time the image flashes in my mind, I see a little more of the person's legs."

"Perhaps you will soon see the person's face," Finch said hopefully.

Jenna stood up. "I can't stay here and let Angie go home alone."

"Why don't I go?" Finch said. "Miss Angie will be upset if you miss the event. These sorts of things aren't for me. Too crowded, too loud. I would be much happier sitting in the family room with Miss Angie sipping some tea."

"Are you sure, Mr. Finch? I'd feel better if she wasn't alone."

Finch smiled. "It would be a great relief to me to have an excuse to leave."

"I'll drive you back," Jenna said. "Oh, Angie took my car."

"I'll get a cab out front. No worries. I'll tell Miss Betty." The man chuckled. "She'll be happy to stay and work the crowd."

"I'll walk you to the lobby, Mr. Finch." Jenna took the man's arm and the two headed to the front of the resort together.

22

A ngie changed out of her evening gown and into a pair of Ellie's pajamas, took two aspirins, and then pulled down the covers and crawled into the comfy bed with her laptop. The cats curled up next to her.

Resting back on the big pillows, Angie's mind wandered over the clues and details of the case, thinking and rethinking about what she knew.

Poor Elizabeth Winters. So much loss in a short time. Had the woman's tethers to reality let go and sent her into a spiral of strange behavior and murder? Angie couldn't believe that. But the boots in her closet. Did she go hiking or did she wear them when she peeped into people's windows and killed Bella Masters?

Then there was Lance. He had similar boots, he was quiet and aloof, he'd suffered by seeing his mother murdered. That might have been enough to send him over the edge. Angie frowned. There was something about Lance though. He seemed to have a calm manner, he seemed kind. She couldn't see him killing anyone.

A thought popped into Angie's mind. Marvin Oates. The man was odd, secretive, he seemed to enjoy putting women down, he planted the idea in Angie's mind that a woman was responsible for the crimes in town.

Oates had even implied that Elizabeth might be the Peeping Tom.

Angie flipped open her laptop. She tapped at the keys and waited for the information to come up. Clicking on one of the articles, she sucked in a breath.

The story reported on Joseph Marvin Oates of South Lisbon, New Jersey, arrested for trespassing in several residents' yards.

Angie's heart pounded. *Joseph Marvin Oates?* It probably wasn't the same person as the man staying at the B and B.

She closed the story and opened the next one.

Joseph M. Oates filed for bankruptcy in Millfield, New Jersey. A different news article reported that Joseph Marvin Oates had been arrested for domestic violence against his girlfriend who later declined to press charges.

Another report of a man of the same name had been investigated in a case of domestic violence.

As sweat beaded up on Angie's forehead, Euclid stood up and moved closer to the young woman, sensing her distress.

"What's going on?" she asked the orange boy. Angie thought about the altercation Oates had with Jenna when she was cleaning his room. He overreacted to a simple misunderstanding, raised his voice, and was hostile to Jenna. Ellie told her the man's credit card didn't go through. *Oh, gosh. Is the Peeping Tom Marvin Oates?*

Angie hit the keys to search for a Marvin Oates in Washington, D.C. since that's where Oates claimed to be from. No one came up who was the same age as the man who was renting a room at the B and B. Not one single person.

Angie's heart dropped into her stomach.

She looked to the side table for her phone to make a call to Chief Martin. *Where's my phone?* As she pushed the blanket back to get out of bed and go downstairs to the kitchen to find her phone, she thought she heard the door to Oates's room open and close.

He's back from the gala at the resort? Angie froze.

JENNA DANCED with Tom and loved being in his arms, but she could not shake the anxiety that pulled at her. The song ended and they walked over to Ellie and Jack who stood near the huge glass windows. A table was set in the corner with ten gingerbread houses. The guests had been asked to cast their ballots for their favorite and the winner would win one thousand dollars for the charity of their choice.

"You look terrible," Ellie told her sister.

Jenna frowned. "Thanks a lot."

"I mean you have worry written all over your face."

"That's because I'm filled with worry. I feel like I'm going to jump out of my skin."

Ellie's muscles tightened. "Is something wrong with Angie?"

"It's not that. I feel like I'm right at the edge of figuring out this mess." Jenna wrung her hands together and as she glanced at the gingerbread houses on the table, her vision dimmed. One house was a Victorian, not unlike the one that belonged to the family.

Blinking, Jenna stared at the house. A ring of fire showed in her vision and formed over the little front door made of cookies. The noise in the ballroom faded until everything was silent. The door to the gingerbread house opened. Angie lay unconscious on the foyer floor. Gigi knelt beside her.

Someone stood on the staircase wearing boots.

Jenna raised her eyes, up, up, and then she saw the person's face.

She saw it.

Jenna opened her eyes and found herself wrapped in Tom's arms. He was sitting in a chair holding her, with Ellie and Jack standing next to them looking alarmed.

"Jenna," his kind voice spoke to his wife. "Can you hear me?"

Ellie held her sister's hand. "Jenna? Are you okay?"

Pushing herself up straighter, Jenna rubbed her aching forehead. "I saw him. I saw him," she mumbled. "Get Chief Martin. Send a police car to the house. Call Angie. Warn her," the young woman babbled.

~

ANGIE SLIPPED out of bed and put her ear to the bedroom door to listen if someone was in the hall. Euclid and Circe jumped off the bed and padded over. Angie raised a finger to her lips. "Shhh."

Footsteps on the stairs, coming up. The cats looked at Angie.

Feet moved across the landing to the room across from Ellie's. A key jangled. The door opened. Elizabeth?

Angie debated leaving the room and heading down to the kitchen for her phone, but was afraid that the person she'd heard a few minutes earlier go into his room might be Oates. What if Elizabeth and Oates are working together?

Angie made a decision, grabbed the knob, and flung the door open. With the cats at her feet, they raced down the staircase to the kitchen.

Breathing hard, Angie looked on every surface in the room. No phone. She let out a groan.

A voice spoke at the entrance to the room. "Ellie?"

Elizabeth Winters came into the kitchen. "Oh, is Ellie here? Her bedroom door was open upstairs."

"It was me. I was in Ellie's room." Angie's face blanched when she saw what Elizabeth was holding.

With a worried expression, Elizabeth stepped forward, took a quick glance behind her, and moved a few more steps closer to Angie. "These were in my closet." The woman held a pair of muddy boots. "They aren't mine. They were under a blanket in the corner of the closet in my room. I think Marvin Oates went into my room and hid these in there."

"Why?" Angie swallowed wondering if this was a trick of some kind. "Why would he do that?"

Elizabeth said, "When I came up the stairs the other morning, I caught him outside my door. My door was open, he looked like he was about to go in. I know I locked it when I left. Oates must have picked the lock or something. I confronted him. He said he knew I was just another crazy female, he said other nutty things. I pushed past him and slammed my door in his face. It was very upsetting."

Setting the boots on the floor, Elizabeth sank into one of the kitchen chairs. "Oates was at the gala this evening. He rushed up to me when he spotted me and started talking crazy again. I told him never to go near my door again. He looked like he might strike me, so I hurried away and came back to the B and B."

Elizabeth took another worried glance over her shoulder. "He must have gone into my room and put these boots in my closet. I think he's trying to make it look like I killed that woman, that I'm the Peeping Tom. I think he's in his room right now. Should I call the police?"

Angie could feel the blood draining out of her head. *This is it. This is the danger we've worried about. It's going to happen. Now. Right now.*

Angie dashed across the room to the kitchen island and pulled out a knife.

Elizabeth's eyes widened with fright and she leapt to her feet. "What are you doing?"

The quickest access to Jenna's car was through the front door. Angie snatched up the car keys, grabbed Elizabeth's arm, and tugged her along down the hallway. "We're getting out of here."

Reaching the foyer, Angie halted so fast that Elizabeth almost tumbled to the floor. Catching herself from falling, the woman looked up and gasped.

Marvin Oates stood in front of the door. He held a long-blade knife. "I was only going to kill *her*. She knows I'm the one. She knows I killed that woman." Oates used his chin to nod at Elizabeth and then the man looked at Angie with wild eyes. "But now I have to kill you, too."

With her heart about to burst through her chest, Angie slowly stepped in front of Elizabeth to protect her ... and then tightened her grip on the knife she took from the kitchen.

23

Jenna was almost screaming now. "Call Angie. Tell her its Oates. Tell her to hide in Ellie's bedroom and lock the door. Where's Chief Martin? We have to get to the Victorian."

Courtney came up to them and when she saw the look on Jenna's face, her breath caught in her throat. "What's going on?"

Jenna shouted. "It's Oates. Angie's at home. We have to go home. Call Angie."

Courtney lifted her hand to show them the phone she was holding. "Angie left her phone on the table."

"My sister!" Jenna screamed, kicked her heels off, and bolted for the hallway.

"Give me the keys to your van," Tom shouted at Ellie.

"I'm going with you." Ellie dashed for her purse and ran for the exit with Tom, Jack, Courtney, and Rufus right behind her. "Someone text Chief Martin. Tell him to send a police car to the Victorian."

When they caught up to Jenna, she shouted, "Call Mr. Finch. Tell him to find Angie and hide."

They ran across the parking lot to Ellie's van and piled in. Jenna, in tears, took the front passenger seat and pounded on the dashboard with her fist. "Go! Go! Go!"

Ellie hit the gas and the van peeled out, roared out of the lot, and tore up the street.

"Don't you die, Angie," Jenna sobbed. "Don't you die."

Standing before Marvin Oates, Angie's mind flew to the description Jenna had given of her little daughter. In a single moment of despair and hopelessness, Angie almost crumpled to the floor. Hot tears burned her eyes. *I'll never see you, Gigi. I'll never know you.*

Elizabeth whimpered and the sound brought

Angie back from the brink of giving up. Rage flared in her chest and boiled her blood. Sweat poured down her back.

No. She glared at Oates. *You won't decide our future.*

Angie attempted to grab for time. "You put those boots in Elizabeth's closet?"

"Clever, right?" Oates grinned crazily.

"How'd you get into her room?"

"I stole the master key from your sister's office. I had a copy made. Then I dropped the one I stole out by the fire pit so it looked like your dumb sister lost it."

"That was you that night standing under the tree looking up at the carriage house apartment?"

"It sure was. Your brother-in-law is pretty slow. It was so easy to outrun him. Maybe he should work out more."

Angie leveled her eyes at the man. "You killed Bella Masters?"

Oates snorted. "She deserved it. That witch pulled a gun on me."

"Like you're pulling a knife on me?"

"You deserve to die, too." Oates blustered.

"Why? What have I done to you?"

"You know what I did."

"Other people know."

"Who?"

"My whole family. They just figured it out. They texted me." Unaware that the family *had* figured it out, Angie thought she was lying to the man. "They're coming here."

Oates narrowed his eyes. "Liar."

"My daughter is here, too," Angie said.

Confusion washed over Oates's face. "You don't have a daughter."

"But, I will." Angie locked eyes with Oates, turned her head slightly towards the woman behind her and whispered, "Run. Now."

Elizabeth hesitated.

"Go," Angie shouted.

The woman wheeled and took off down the hall … and her rush to escape made Marvin Oates leap forward.

ELLIE WHIPPED the van around the corner onto Beach Street and pulled to a halt in front of the Victorian. Jenna reached for the car door handle, but Tom, sitting behind her, put his hand on her shoulder.

"Hold up," he said. "Let's be smart. There are six of us. Let's make a plan."

~

ANGIE STEPPED to the side to block Oates's attempt to go after Elizabeth, then she bent her knees and raised the knife.

Oates changed direction, lifted his own hand with the knife in it, and charged at Angie. The blade glanced off Angie's arm, but she side-stepped and slashed Oates across the face with a fierce blow.

Something moved in her peripheral vision.

Finch, with his cane held above his head, rushed, limping, into the foyer and bashed Oates over the shoulder. The older man dropped to the floor and rolled into Oates's legs, knocking the man off-balance. Oates stumbled into the foyer Christmas tree, knocking it over.

Two things flew past Angie's line of sight. One black and one orange.

The cats leapt onto Oates's back, scratching, clawing, and hissing.

When Oates fell to the ground, screaming, he dropped his knife and Angie scurried to grab it.

Several B and B guests raced to the second floor

landing to see what was going on downstairs and when they saw the fight below, screams rang out. One man ran for his phone to call the police.

The front door flew open and Tom, carrying a tire iron, Jenna, and Ellie dashed into the foyer. At the same time, the rear flank advanced from the hallway as Rufus, with a bat, Courtney, with a kitchen knife, and Jack carrying the poker from the fire pit, raced forward.

Dazed, Mr. Finch sat next to the fallen tree. Courtney hurried to see if he was alright.

Angie lay on her back, a knife in each of her hands, her arm bleeding onto the wood floor. When she saw the family, armed and ready, the corners of her mouth went up into a little smile.

A police car's siren could be heard through the open front door.

Euclid and Circe dashed over to check on Angie and gently touched her with their paws.

"My heroes," Angie whispered ... and then a flood of tears let loose when Jenna knelt and wrapped her sister in her arms.

RACING THROUGH THE DOOR, Josh spotted Jenna

holding Angie on the foyer floor. His face paled and his stomach lurched thinking his fiancée was hurt, or worse. Falling to his knees, he saw Angie's blue eyes open and tears glistening on her cheeks.

Angie reached for Josh and the two embraced.

"Are you hurt?"

"I'm fine." Angie's voice was weak.

"I would have left the resort to come back here with you." Josh ran his hand over Angie's dark blond hair and hugged her to his chest. "Nothing is more important to me than you."

Two squad cars had arrived and Marvin Oates was subdued by the officers, although Mr. Finch, Angie, and the cats had already seen to that. The man was handcuffed and removed from house.

Elizabeth Winters was in the living room being questioned by an officer. As she ran from the Victorian at Angie's order, she'd run right into Rufus, Jack, and Courtney who were sneaking in the back way. Courtney instructed the woman to hide in Ellie's van until they gave the *all clear.*

Chief Martin was the next one through the front door of the house, his face strained with worry and concern and when he saw everyone, unhurt, present and accounted for, the tension drained from his muscles.

It was a sight to behold with Angie, Josh, Jenna, and Tom clustered together inside the door, the tall Christmas tree prone on the floor, decorations broken and askew, Finch and Courtney sitting near the bottom of the staircase, B and B guests hanging over the upstairs railing watching the proceedings, Ellie at the top of the stairs assuring the guests that all was now well, Jack and Rufus bringing ice, towels, and glasses of water to Finch and Angie, and the two fine felines moving from person to person to give them licks on the hands or faces.

"Everyone's okay?" the chief asked.

"We're all great," Courtney said to the chief from her position on the floor with her arm around Finch's shoulders. "Just another evening with the family."

The group couldn't help but chuckle.

An ambulance arrived and the EMTs checked the slash on Angie's arm from Oates's knife and also tended to Mr. Finch whose bad leg had been twisted in his attack on Oates. On the advice of the EMTs, Angie and Finch rode to the hospital in the ambulance to be more fully examined.

"I'll go as long as Mr. Finch and I can ride together," Angie said.

Placed on gurneys, Angie and Finch had reached

their arms out to each other and held hands as they were transported to the waiting ambulance.

"I should have gotten to the house sooner, Miss Angie. I took a cab from the resort to my house, got some clothes to change out of my tux, and walked over. When I came in through the back way, Euclid and Circe met me in the kitchen, fussing and hissing. I knew something was terribly wrong and followed the cats to the hall. I heard you talking to Oates. That's when I raised my cane and charged."

"Thank you, Mr. Finch." Angie looked tenderly at the older man and squeezed his hand. "You're always there for me."

Josh and Jenna followed the ambulance by car and waited for Angie and Finch to be evaluated while the rest of the family stayed at the house to clean up the mess in the foyer and right the tree.

Betty arrived at the hospital in a tizzy and when she saw Finch on the bed in the emergency room, she nearly smothered him, her grip on the man was so tight. "Victor. Thank the heavens. I should never leave your side." She covered Finch with kisses and the man's cheeks flushed bright red.

The doctor closed Angie's wound with a few stitches. Finch had sprained the knee on his bad leg and was fitted with a brace to wear until the joint recovered.

Before Betty helped Finch to her car, Angie and the older man embraced for a long time in front of the emergency room's exit doors.

Finch whispered, "I intend to live long enough to see little Gigi and help her grow up."

"You and me, both." Angie said softly and hugged the man tighter.

Finch tenderly touched Angie's cheek, gave her a nod, and then walked with Betty to her car.

While Jenna drove back to the house, Angie sat in the backseat of the car leaning against Josh, their hands holding tightly together.

24

Holiday tunes played over the bake shop speakers to a full house of people joyful and relieved to have the Peeping Tom in custody. The townspeople came and went all day long to give Angie their good wishes and to tell her how glad they were that she had emerged nearly unscathed from the terrible man's attack.

"I hope he's in prison for the rest of his awful life," one person said.

"Thanks to you, the monster has finally been caught," another Sweet Cove resident told Angie.

The customers enjoyed coffees, teas, smoothies, and hot chocolates along with different holiday sweets, muffins, cookies, and slices of pies and cakes.

"We have so much to be thankful for," a bake shop regular told a small group.

As the afternoon went on, the crowd thinned and Angie worked in the kitchen for an hour while Louisa handled the customers. Carrying a platter of sticky buns to the glass case, Angie saw Louisa standing by one of the café tables chatting with someone. When she stepped a little to the side, she could see Lance sitting at the table with a cup of coffee smiling up at the pretty, dark-haired, young woman.

Lance said something to Louisa and she turned and waved Angie over.

"Lance has something to tell you."

Angie gave Lance a smile and greeted him.

Lance looked down at the table.

"Tell her," Louisa encouraged the young man. "I can promise you that Angie doesn't bite. At least, not too often."

A shy smile lifted Lance's lips. He took a swallow of his coffee and cleared his throat. "My grand-mother is a terrific baker ... just like you." He paused and looked up at Angie. "She read about you in the newspaper a while back. She thinks you are a great person for helping people."

"That's really nice of her," Angie smiled.

"Gram has an old book, it's full of recipes she put

together over the years, a lot of them she came up with herself. She wants me to give you the book of recipes. Gram says she won't be on this earth forever and she wants you to have the book."

Angie's eyes went wide. "Really? That's so kind of her. But, what about you, Lance? Don't you want to keep it?"

Lance shook his head. "It should go to a real baker. Anyway, Gram has already copied all the recipes into a new book for me to have." Lance grinned. "She says maybe one of these days, I'll want to bake something. I'm not sure about that."

"Tell your Gram that I'll cherish the book."

"I have it in my truck. I'll go get it."

Watching the young man leave the bake shop, Angie realized that the news clipping in Lance's toolbox must have been from his grandmother. She must have given it to him when he told her he was working at the Victorian.

"He's cute, isn't he?" Louisa gushed.

Angie gave her a look. "Do I sense someone has a crush?"

"Yes, you do." Louisa's smile was a like a thousand-watt bulb. "And guess what? Someone has a crush on me."

"Is that so?" Angie asked with a twinkle in her eye.

"Lance has had a tough life. He's suffered an awful loss and seen some things no one should ever see, but he's kind and honest and sweet. He's also fun and we get along really well."

"I'm glad," Angie said. "It makes me happy ... for both of you."

Lance came back in and handed Angie a book wrapped in brown paper and tied with a piece of string.

Angie opened it and turned some of the hand-written pages to look over the recipes. "These are wonderful, thank you so much. I'd love to send your grandmother a note, if you could give me her address."

The three sat down at the café table and chatted together, the little candles in the bake shop's windows glowing warmly as the day's light began to wane.

~

WHILE JENNA WORKED at her desk on a new jewelry design, her mind replayed the events of the past weeks and she shuddered at the close call that

Angie had with Marvin Oates. Thinking about the clues and how they'd tried to figure it all out, she considered some things they should have picked up on.

Sighing, she knew that it was easy to look back and now see what had been right in front of them, but at the time, so much seemed like a jumble that it was hard to tease out the threads from the mess of it.

When Jenna stretched her arms over her head, the cats sat up on the sofa and trilled. Looking over at them, she noticed they were both staring at the small Christmas tree in the corner of the shop.

The lights on the tree glowed brightly and then the different colors of light sparkled and lifted and swirled in the air until a flash nearly blinded Jenna.

When she opened her eyes, Jenna's heart did a flip.

Her nana's spirit was glimmering next to the tree. Nana sat in a wooden rocking chair, moving gently back and forth.

Gigi cuddled on Nana's lap, wrapped comfortably in her great-grandmother's arms.

The two spirits made eye contact with Jenna and smiled warmly at her filling the young woman's heart with love.

Gigi lifted her hand and waved, and then the two

spirits, one from the past and one from the future, glittered and faded and disappeared.

A happy tear rolled down Jenna's cheek and Euclid and Circe lifted their little noses in the air and trilled.

25

A light snow fell in the frigid air of Sweet Cove, but inside the Victorian a fire blazed in the living room fireplace, Ellie played holiday songs on the piano with Jack, Tom, and Jenna singing along at the top of their lungs. The cats sat on the baby grand piano, howling away as part of the chorus.

Betty, Chief Martin, and the chief's wife, Lucille, enjoyed drinks and hors d'oeuvres while sitting on the sofa and chairs chatting together and occasionally joining in on one of the carols.

The foyer tree had been righted and Courtney and Rufus worked to re-decorate it with glass ornaments and red bows. Listening to the singing coming from the living room, Courtney nodded to the performers and then said to Rufus, "I hope the neighbors don't call the police thinking all that noise is someone being murdered in here."

"We can only hope." Rufus put his fingers in his ears to joke.

Angie and Josh were setting the table with the red and green plates, crystal goblets, and silverware. It was a week before Christmas and the family decided to have everyone over for dinner to celebrate the end of the Peeping Tom's crime spree.

Finch's knee still need to be babied, but he wanted to be as active and helpful as possible so he assisted with the table by carrying wine glasses from the China cabinet to each place setting.

Courtney came in to get another box of decorations that she'd left in the dining room. "Did you bring your sketchbook, Mr. Finch?"

"Indeed, I did, Miss Courtney."

"Mr. Finch has been doing more drawing. Maybe Jenna will have more visions and see something in the new pictures."

Angie and Josh exchanged glances.

"Let's hope not," Angie said.

Courtney said, "If it didn't have to do with crimes, it would be kind of cool if Jenna could still see things that aren't actually drawn into Mr. Finch's artwork. Maybe she could practice and eventually see the week's lottery numbers before they're drawn."

Mr. Finch grinned. "One never knows what hidden skills he or she might have."

"I wonder if Nana will come back someday?" Courtney looked through the box of decorations.

"I would bet on it," Finch said.

"We already know we'll see Gigi one day." Courtney smiled at Angie and Josh. "You two need to pick the wedding date. That little girl doesn't want to wait forever to be born, you know."

Angie and Josh ignored the youngest Roseland sister.

"It was so cool how different spirits came to help us." Courtney pulled a silver angel from the box. "It was like that Scrooge story where spirits visit him from the past, present, and future. We had the same thing. Nana came from the past, Gigi came from the future, and Mr. Finch and Jenna were the helpers from the present."

Josh looked over at Angie and said quietly, "That *is* pretty cool, isn't it?"

The doorbell rang and Rufus answered.

Louisa and Lance entered the foyer, both dressed up for the occasion with Louisa in a bright red dress with black heels and Lance in a fitted dark blue suit.

She handed Rufus a platter covered with a glass dome. "We used one of Lance's grandmother's dessert recipes and made a cheesecake."

When the table was finished, everyone congregated in the living room until the dinner of stew and roasted vegetables was finished cooking in the oven. The fire warmed the room and candles flickered on the coffee table and side tables.

Ellie and Jack sat side by side on the piano stool playing duets and chatting with the others.

"Elizabeth Winters went back to Boston today," Ellie told them.

"I had another chance to speak with her before she left," the chief said. "She's going to start grief counseling after the holidays to help her cope with the loss of her husband and mother."

"Does she have anyone to spend the holidays with?" Jenna asked, concerned about the woman being alone.

"She'll be staying with her sister and her sister's family." The chief nodded. "Elizabeth told me that Marvin Oates frequently harassed her while they were both staying here in town. He said annoying things to her and seemed to take pleasure in being challenging and rude to her. Oates was sure that Elizabeth had found him out and he'd pass her and say things like ... *you'll never prove its me* or *I'll pin it all on you.* She thought he was crazy and didn't attribute his comments to the crimes until she found the boots he'd planted in her room. People never think the folks around them could ever be criminals."

"Except for us," Courtney said, "we suspect everyone."

The group chuckled.

Chief Martin reached for a large gift bag. "In the spirit of the holidays, I have something for some of you. The things aren't gifts. They're tokens of my esteem and thanks ... and will probably come in handy in the future." He dug into the bag and removed a small, wrapped box with a red bow on top. "This is for you, Courtney."

Courtney let out a little whoop and hurried over to the chief. "What is it?"

"You'll have to open it to find out."

Carefully removing the wrapping, Courtney gave the chief a look and a smile, and then removed the lid from the box. A screech of delight filled the air as the young woman broke into a spontaneous dance.

"What in the world is it?" Ellie asked.

Courtney stood still and looked in the box again. Her eyes glistened with moisture and she wrapped her arms around Chief Martin. "I can't believe it. Thank you."

"You'd better show us what's in that box," Jenna demanded with smile.

Courtney held it out for everyone to see.

Inside the box, on a bed of black velvet, was a silver badge with a small star engraved at the top of it. The words, *Sweet Cove Police Department – Consultant* were etched around the top edge of the badge. Her name was engraved on the bottom.

Courtney gave the chief another hug and then pinned the badge onto her dress.

"There's a leather holder in the box, too," the chief said, "in case you just want to flash it at people."

"You never told me how all of you have been trained in criminal consultation." Rufus admired the badge.

"It's quite a long story," Courtney told her boyfriend. "I'll tell you one day." She winked at the chief.

Chief Martin removed boxes from the bag and handed them to Angie, Ellie, Jenna, and Mr. Finch. The four of them opened the boxes to find their own Sweet Cove Police Consultant badges.

"I thought we should make it official," the chief

said. "To make sure you have proper identification when you assist on cases." The chief smiled at Courtney. "Courtney's is the only one that has a star engraved on it. She's badgered me about getting a silver sheriff's star since you all started helping me with cases. I thought it was time."

The chief looked over at Euclid and Circe. "I also thought about getting you two badges as well, but I didn't know how you'd pin them on."

Euclid shook his orange plume of a tail and meowed.

After dinner, the group played charades, sang carols, and then had tea and cheesecake for dessert.

Ellie said, "I've been thinking about something. I've been thinking about running for office."

Everyone stared.

"Elected office?" Angie asked.

"Yes. Jack and I have been discussing it. The seat Bella Masters held on the town finance committee needs to be filled. I have an understanding of financial matters and I'm a quick learner. Dr. Masters was an intelligent, principled, hardworking, and accomplished woman. I'd be thrilled to serve the town in her honor."

"Wow," Jenna said admiringly. "That's fantastic."

"Perhaps this will lead to other ways to serve,

Miss Ellie," Finch said. "One day, you might become a state senator or a United States Senator." Finch winked. "Or maybe someday, something even higher."

"What's the next step to take to run?" Josh asked.

Ellie said, "I don't actually have to run this time because the seat will be filled by appointing someone, due to Dr. Masters's passing. I need to submit my letter of intention and my resume and then all candidates will be interviewed."

"This is exciting," Courtney said, her eyes beaming. "I hope they choose you."

"Me, too," Ellie said as she took Jack's hand in hers. "Jack is going to do mock interviews with me to help me prepare. I really want to serve on the committee."

After everyone wished Ellie well and offered to help her in any way they could, Josh cleared his throat. "Angie and I have an announcement to make."

All eyes turned to the couple.

"Did you finally...?" Courtney's eyes were wide and she leaned forward eagerly waiting for Josh to speak.

"I couldn't wait to marry this woman any longer,"

Josh smiled broadly at his sweetheart. "We've set our wedding date."

"It will be in the spring," Angie said happily. "It will be in the evening on the third Saturday in May."

Euclid and Circe let out meows of approval, and applause and whoops filled the air as hugs and handshakes went around the room.

"Angie is the best person I've ever met and I can't wait to spend the rest of my life with her." Josh wrapped his arms around the honey blond and pulled her close … in the room lit by the warm glow of the fire, the candles, and the lights of the glittering Christmas tree, and in the loving company of their family and friends … and two fine felines.

THANK YOU FOR READING! RECIPES BELOW!

Books by J.A. WHITING can be found here:
www.amazon.com/author/jawhiting

To hear about new books and book sales, please sign up for my mailing list at:
www.jawhitingbooks.com

Your email will never be sold, shared, or spammed.

If you enjoyed the book, please consider leaving a review. A few words are all that's needed. It would be very much appreciated.

BOOKS/SERIES BY J. A. WHITING

CLAIRE ROLLINS COZY MYSTERY SERIES

PAXTON PARK COZY MYSTERIES

LIN COFFIN COZY MYSTERY SERIES

SWEET COVE COZY MYSTERY SERIES

OLIVIA MILLER MYSTERY-THRILLER SERIES
(not cozy)

ABOUT THE AUTHOR

J.A. Whiting lives with her family in New England. Whiting loves reading and writing mystery stories.

Visit me at:
www.jawhitingbooks.com/
www.facebook.com/jawhitingauthor
www.amazon.com/author/jawhiting

SOME RECIPES FROM THE SWEET COVE SERIES

HOLIDAY CHOCOLATE FUDGE

<u>INGREDIENTS</u>

2½ cups semisweet chocolate chips

2 cups miniature marshmallows

14 ounces sweetened condensed milk

1½ teaspoons vanilla

1 cup chopped nuts (optional)

½ cup dried cherries or dried apricots (chopped)

⅓ cup white baking chips, melted

<u>DIRECTIONS</u>

Grease sides and bottom of a square pan (9 X 9 X 2 inches).

Heat chocolate chips, marshmallows, and condensed milk in a saucepan over medium heat;

stir constantly until the ingredients are melted and the mixture is smooth .

Stir in vanilla, nuts (if desired), and cherries or apricots and then pour into the greased pan.

Drizzle with melted white baking chips.

Cover and refrigerate for about 2 hours or until the fudge is firm.

Cut into 1-inch squares.

OATMEAL AND BUTTERSCOTCH COOKIES

INGREDIENTS

1⅓ cups all-purpose flour

1 teaspoon baking soda

½ teaspoon salt

¾ teaspoon ground cinnamon

2 sticks butter, softened

½ cup granulated sugar

¾ cup packed brown sugar

2 large eggs

1 teaspoon vanilla

3 cups old-fashioned or quick oats

1⅔ cups butterscotch chips

DIRECTIONS

Preheat the oven to 375 degrees F.

Combine flour, baking soda, salt, and cinnamon in a bowl.

Beat butter, sugar, brown sugar, eggs, and vanilla in a large mixing bowl.

Slowly beat in the flour mixture until well-blended.

Stir in oats and butterscotch chips.

Drop rounded tablespoons of dough onto ungreased cookie sheets.

For chewy cookies, bake for about 8 minutes; for more crispy cookies, bake for about 10 minutes.

Cool on cookie sheet for about 3-4 minutes.

Move to wire rack to fully cool.

CHOCOLATE-PEPPERMINT CHEESECAKE

INGREDIENTS

FILLING

3 8-ounce blocks cream cheese, softened

2 cups granulated sugar

2 large eggs

⅓ cup sour cream

1½ tablespoons flour

1 teaspoon peppermint extract

1 teaspoon vanilla

¼ teaspoon kosher salt

½ cup chopped chocolate, plus 2 tablespoons to use as garnish

½ cup chopped white chocolate, plus 2 tablespoons to use as garnish

½ cup chopped candy canes, plus 2 tablespoons to use as garnish

OREO CRUST

24 peppermint oreos
6 tablespoons melted butter

CHOCOLATE GANACHE

¾ cup warmed heavy cream
1½ cups semisweet chocolate chips

DIRECTIONS

Preheat the oven to 350 degrees F.

Spray a 9 inch springform pan with cooking spray.

FILLING

In a large bowl, beat cream cheese and sugar.

Add eggs, one at a time.

Add in sour cream, flour, peppermint extract, vanilla, and salt.

Fold in chopped chocolate, white chocolate, and candy canes.

Set aside.

CRUST

In a large plastic bag, crush the oreos into fine crumbs (or use a food processor).

Stir together with melted butter until moist.

Place the crust in the prepared pan and pack well.

Pour the filling over the crust.

Place the springform pan on a baking sheet.

Bake for about 1 hour, until the middle is only a bit jiggly.

Turn off the oven and let the cheesecake cool in the oven for about 45 minutes.

Refrigerate the cheesecake until chilled – 4-5 hours, but best if chilled overnight.

CHOCOLATE GANACHE

Pour heated cream over chocolate chips – let sit for 5 minutes.

Stir well until all the chocolate is melted – if it appears too thin, then refrigerate for 5 minutes.

Spread the ganache over the cheesecake.

Garnish with chopped chocolate and candy canes.

Refrigerate for 10 minutes before serving until the ganache hardens.

APPLE AND CRANBERRY PIE

*Use your favorite recipe for the pie crusts

INGREDIENTS

FILLING

    1 cup sweetened dried cranberries

    ½ cup sugar

    2 tablespoons all purpose flour

    ½ teaspoon ground cinnamon

    2¼ pounds of apples sliced into ¼ inch slices (need about 7 cups of apple slices – can use a mix of Granny Smith, Golden or Red Delicious, Gala, Fuji, McIntosh, Cortland, Empire)

    1 teaspoon brandy

1 teaspoon vanilla

EGG WASH
1 large egg yolk
1 tablespoon whipping cream

DIRECTIONS
Preheat the oven to 375 degrees F – the rack should be in the bottom third of the oven.

APPLE FILLING
In a large bowl, whisk together sugar, flour, and cinnamon.

Add the cranberries and coat them with the mixture.

Add the apples, toss to coat.

Sprinkle with brandy and vanilla.

PIE
Roll out your favorite pie dough and place into a 9-inch glass pie dish; press down.

Place the apple filling into the pie dish.

Roll out the top crust; top the pie; crimp the edges.

Brush Pie with the Egg Wash – In a bowl, whisk together egg yolk and cream to blend; use a pastry brush and brush the egg wash over the top of the pie.

Cut slices into top crust with sharp knife so steam can escape while baking.

Bake the pie in the 375 degree F oven for 30 minutes.

Place aluminum foil over the pie and lower the temperature to 350 degrees F and bake for another 45 – 55 minutes until the apples are tender and the top of the crust is golden.

Enjoy !

Made in the USA
Las Vegas, NV
30 October 2023

79942789R00157